A Thousand Miles
of Road

A story collection

by Joseph Kraus

A Thousand Miles of Road

Copyright © 2025 by Joseph Kraus

Cover image © by Jack Kraus

First Printing: August 2025

Published by **DarkWinter Press**: www.darkwinterlit.com

ISBN: 978-1-998441-29-7

For my wife. Nobody has ever believed in me so much.

Table of Contents

The Love Store

I

"What does your honey like?" Melanie's voice was like a wisp of conversation from another room that slips under the crack of a door, something you had to strain to make out and never were sure what you'd heard. The bend in her words made people think she grew up somewhere down south and far away from the frozen sidewalks outside.

The guy wore a sweater zipped up so tightly that it would leave notches in his neck when he took it off that evening. His hair cut was so fresh the clippings must've still been prickling on his neck, and his own face still unrecognizable in the mirror, an alien unto himself.

For 30 minutes now he had been circumnavigating the store, removing the costume necklaces from the metal trees and letting each one dangle off his hooked finger before putting it back, rotating the bracelets around the velvet-covered rod to get a look at every glass stone before moving on, and forever spinning the turnstiles like a kid who wants nothing more than to hear the chittery earrings and send the brooches shooting out in every direction. Thirty minutes in a store as dinky as Love Tokens was enough time to wear the carpet down to foam. Just couldn't make up his mind. His honey was one of those.

He flinched at the sound of her voice, knocking from the ridge of his nose the billboard-sized plastic glasses just as suited for seeing as for blocking out flying debris from power tools. He must not have noticed her poised behind the glass display case, barely existing in the endless dead lull of the weeks between Christmas and Valentine's Day, the store only scratching along on the scraps of a few birthdays and the rare anniversaries of people who got married in January, most of them the result of surprise pregnancies which couldn't wait on spring. There she was, so long waiting for anybody to come in, her head framed by a column of clutch purses on one side and scarves feathering down the other. He looked her way, but didn't reply, the reaction of a man exploring the relics of a condemned arcade when the swami inside the glass booth erupts to life from the darkness, barking an offer of a fortune if he only drops a nickel in the slot.

She had to speak again to break his petrification, his hand fingering a pair of danglers that he must've reconsidered and dismissed five times already. "What's her taste in sparkle?" She was the one putting the nickel in now, hoping he could give her some useful information to go on. "What's she like? Your honey?"

"Honey." He said the word like he'd just learned it in some evening French class and would recite it over and over throughout the evening, only to forget the meaning and pronunciation by tomorrow. "Oh, she—" He let the earrings drop between his fingers and poked the hefty glasses back onto his head, something he'd done a dozen times during his search, nothing but an involuntary reflex anymore, only noticed by the people around him who must've frequently imagined smashing those glasses of his with a ball peen hammer just to stop the endless anticipation of him righting them. He found the earrings again. "I'm not too sure."

Melanie came off her stool from behind the display case, rounded the novelty rack of hand-painted flasks for the girl who just needed a nip in her purse to get her through the day, and waded her way over to where he was drowning in so much glitter and glass. "Does she like them to stay put when she walks or brush her neck?" She pointed toward two choices, one for the demure and one for the splashy, but when she noticed the lumpy veins squirming on the back of her hand, she quickly rotated it so her palm faced him. God, those hands. No cream was going to stop the blood from flowing, reverse so many years of scrubbing out sinks and bathtubs at the Holloway Inn before cleaning ladies ever thought to wear gloves, the Ajax raking the skin right off her hands until she went home each night with them as red and blazing as peeled away blisters. Two decades later and those hands still hadn't recovered; they out-aged the rest of her by fifteen years, could've been hands clawing their way up from the grave.

He tilted his head on shrugging shoulders, couldn't even speak to venture a guess.

"Don't know what your girl likes? That's your problem right there." Melanie wore glasses too, and they were probably as big as his, except hers weren't billboards but oyster shells. An inch closer to each other, and they might click together like teeth. If he ever kissed her, one of them would have to take their pair off first to close the distance. "How long have you two been together?" She'd start with that question, work her way in.

"Long enough to know her. *I know her.*" His stress on this last statement caused Melanie to remove her hand from in front of his face and take a slight step back.

"What's the occasion?"

"Her birthday."

Not an anniversary and no ring on this finger. Sometimes you just got stuck in a holding pattern, occupying the same space, the same routines—Chinese take-out every Thursday night, Hearts with the downstairs neighbors on Friday, Love Boat and Fantasy Island on Saturday—comfort in the predictability of one day to the next, but never progressing from there because there were too many things not right—her never liking what she ordered from Kim Lai, acting sour and ruining the game for everybody if the Queen landed in her pile too frequently, or staying awake long enough for Mr. Roarke to bid his guests adieu but letting exhaustion take hold upon their seaplane exit, just too tired tonight if that was okay. It always was. With this boy, it always was. There never seemed enough things wrong to call it quits, nor enough things right to bury a ring in her chocolate mousse and let her chomp right down onto it, easier just to go along always knowing there was really nothing keeping you from packing up and walking out the door if you suddenly couldn't stand it anymore. This shopping trip might finally send this one down the road.

"How old?" She leaned ever so slightly to catch a glimpse of herself in the two inch-wide mirror running along the corner of the turnstile. All she saw was her mouth, her burgundy lipstick turning the chapped cracks into black fissures. Goddamn winters here sucked her dry. She puckered to try to make the pinches at the corners look like they belonged, inching her lips back to see a feather of lip sludge on her front tooth that she concealed with pursed lips and dug at with her tongue. She weaved ever so slightly back and forth to catch more of herself, but there just wasn't enough mirror.

"Thirty-eight."

Only seven years younger than Melanie. He didn't look over thirty-five, even with those glasses that he must've dug out of a Salvation Army bin. Maybe he had hooked up with somebody older, and he was regretting it now, or maybe he was pushing fifty, but she couldn't see the wrinkles because he hadn't moved his face to smile in fifteen years. Even she managed to smile. Even by herself, working every day through January in this grim, forgotten store, she smiled at the people walking by. Why not be happy? Some smiled back.

"Think about when you take her out. Does the way she dresses make you more interested in your food..." She gestured to the string of faux pearls, and then she moved onto a burnished gold number with dainty garnet-colored beads leading down to a teardrop-shaped pendant that would hang perfectly into a cleft of cleavage if his honey had any. "Or make you want to beat down the first guy who looks at her?"

"I don't know." He pushed at the glasses even though they hadn't fallen.

Her guess was that he'd long ago stopped caring. "These are from Germany." She took a safe pair of earrings, not too prudish and not too flashy. "Not emeralds or anything, but they sure could be. No girl wouldn't like to sparkle a little more."

"No, I don't think so. I don't think anything today." He scanned the store one more time, clutching onto a table leg as if so many choices would swirl around him and whisk him up into the neverland of space and stars. The necklaces and bracelets trembled on that table, smacking the light here and there. "To tell you the truth, I don't think she'd like anything in here. She likes real stuff."

"Real stuff, huh?" Melanie said. "Should've gone to Zales in the mall." Her voice spiked, but she corralled it. "Price doesn't denote beauty." For his honey, though, it probably did. She probably checked his credit card statement after every holiday to make sure he loved her enough. There was no accounting for taste. "This is as real as it gets." She wasn't talking about the selection, which needed no defending from her.

"It doesn't have anything to do with your jewelry—"

"It's just her," Melanie said. "I know."

"I thought maybe…I came in here because I don't have much time." He gazed past her out the windows where a mother was hollering at her kids, too small to see, telling them to get away from that curb because the cars were coming, and they were going to get run over. Better listen to Mom on that one. Cars went too fast down this street. One false step, and you could lose one.

The frames had sagged again, and behind them his eyes flickered in the afternoon light like all that German cut glass. "Her birthday's today."

"Waited until last minute."

"I've been looking all week. She can be tough to shop for." He reset his glasses, looking down into them and not at her. "I never get it right. I've been wandering from store to store. I looked in here and thought maybe…"

Maybe he had seen her through those windows, the fortune teller in her glass booth who couldn't possibly know anything about what he was going through, how to make it any better, or how things were going to turn out, but for just a nickel she'd at least tell him something.

"Well, maybe you shouldn't try so hard." Melanie pinched a tuft of hair unfurled from the clipped-up mass, pulled it straight, and released it. She let her fingers dribble onto her shoulder, over the creases of the cotton dress she should've ironed that morning after salvaging it from her crammed closet, and down all the way to the hem just above her knees where her fingers, with nothing left to feel, dropped to her side. In their journey, she felt the pronounced collar

6

bone, the still-upturned curve of her breasts, the corrugation of her ribcage that had been swallowed up by flab in most women her age, and the unshakeable thighs from her mile and a half trek here every morning that she insisted upon even during the dead of winter when her leather shoes took a beating in the salt and slush. "That's not how it's supposed to be. It shouldn't be hard at all."

He had sat himself down on the edge of a table that she wasn't sure would hold him, except right then, he didn't look heavy enough to hold down himself. "I know it's not."

Some gray-haired guy opened the door with a bleep. The wind snapped in from the Nor'easter that was supposed to be arriving tonight. He took a quick look inside the door and shut it again, looking up at the sign to realize he was in the wrong place before moving on. "Wants the bar next door," she said. "Closest thing to another customer I'll have today. You were my last hope, but you're not going to find what you need here." This jewelry was for a woman who appreciated sparkle more than carats, someone who examined the wrapping paper on the box instead of just shredding it to see what was inside, hated to open it at all because holding the wrapped box that someone had gone through the effort to search for and then package up so pretty was more than enough for her, more than a lot of women got on their birthdays. Not his girl. "You aren't going to find anything she likes. Don't bother. How's about you giving me a ride home instead?"

The wind chuttered against the single pane windows. One good gust might blow them in, her left to sweep up mounds of glass afterward, picking through the pile to separate the cut pieces from the ones that would cut her. "No, I can't. I'm supposed to—" He shook his head, and a droplet appeared

7

on the inside of one lens. "I'm supposed to be home. The stores are closing, and it's not just the gift. I got a lot to do."

For the first time, her voice rose above a hush. He wasn't going to be spending in her store, and Jesus, get a backbone. "You're empty handed. I bet she expects dinner too and a cake with candles like she's seven years old again. Maybe some balloons tied to the back of her chair."

He neither confirmed nor denied.

"Jesus. You don't stand a chance. My advice? Stay away as long as possible." He had a shit storm waiting now or later. "Now, you're not going to let a girl get eaten up by this weather? My place isn't far, but it is if I'm walking. I'm not going to beat that storm."

"But I should—" He looked around, but all the glass had absorbed the shadows of the coming evening, as if all she sold here was hematite and onyx. Normally, this was about the time of day she'd switch on the two Tiffany lamps and wait for some stragglers before close. They weren't coming tonight, though. Nobody aside from the gray-haired guy was even braving the weather for a pint and a game of darts next door.

Every year there was talk that Love Tokens would close, or at least her position cut, always in the winter when the days were so short and shoppers so scarce. The outlook had never seemed this bleak before, though. Everybody losing their jobs, and nobody hiring, foreclosure signs clogging up the neighborhood streets. People sure weren't out buying jewelry, even costume pieces, unless they came from Xanadu two blocks over where you could buy a glass bracelet thirty bucks cheaper because it wasn't shipped over from Europe but instead strung together in town by some baked-out hippie girl with a needle, a pile of dime store beads, and a developing case of carpal tunnel. Even if this store did make it to Valentine's

Day, how long could one day keep it going? How long could they keep her around? Pretty soon Carly was going to have to come out of his retirement of gardening and watching daytime game shows to start manning the store again, like the old days when his wife was still around and the two of them did just fine on their own without having to pay any employee.

The guy's face was slack, but he nodded, probably appreciative of having something to do that could take him off the merry-go-round of trying to please someone who couldn't be pleased.

"I'll tell you what," she said. "There's a boutique right near my house. They have these silk scarves that nobody could turn up her nose at, and if she does, just run the silk across her face." The back of her hand became the scarf, floating along his jawbone. He didn't flinch, but held there until her hand traveled from ear to chin, not a prickle of stubble the whole way. Such a little boy. And not at all used to tenderness. "See if she doesn't melt then."

The hand-painted wood sign for Love Tokens rattled above them on corroded nails as she locked up. Who knew if it'd be there tomorrow? The paint was too ratty and faded to be legible anyway. Carly didn't want to pay anybody to touch it up.

The inclement storm had turned the cobble streets into the apocalypse, the two of them the sole survivors. They leaned into the wind with hands clamped in their pockets to keep their coats from being ripped from their bodies, shoulders hunched, and focusing on the stone sidewalks. She opened her mouth to yell something or other over the whirring in their ears, but the wind belted her and punched her words back into her throat, the snatch of cold enough to stop her heart. His car was forever away, probably a quarter of the way back to her

9

apartment. He'd walked a good distance to end up at her store, probably drifted in and out of a half dozen other shops, fingering books, CDs, sweaters, perfume, and knowing all the while it was hopeless.

His Volvo wagon was the only car left along the curb, and as she rounded the car to the passenger side, she peered through the darkened glass into the back seat, looking for booster seats or empty juice boxes or stuffed penguins. It looked empty as far as she could tell. The snow was dusting from the sky, clinging to the car's ridges and collecting along the wiper blades. He unlocked her side first, and she slid into the passenger seat like landing on a slab of ice.

She flipped his lock to let him in and scanned the backseat on her way back to her side. It was as clean as the day it left the lot fifteen or so years ago. If he did have kids, he must've scoured away the evidence each time they left the car.

He turned the key, and air blasted from the vents as if they were in the wind again. He shut off the fan and sat looking at the dash for a moment. The side of his face was chapped from the wind. She wanted to brush her hand over it again to take away the cold, take away the burn. He righted his glasses on his head and glanced over, not at her but at the glove compartment. He had something to say that he'd been saving during the walk here. "Don't think bad about her. She can't help but be disappointed. It's just her thing."

"Oh yeah, they all have their things." She shook her head at him. "You want to know my ex-husband's thing? Disappearing on his way home from work whenever he felt like it, sometimes for hours, sometimes days. Arriving back home without any explanation but all bristly because of it just the same, ready to land a good one on me if I asked where the hell he'd been. But I always did ask, even though I knew what was coming, even though I knew he'd never tell me. I couldn't help but ask. Who couldn't help but ask?"

He didn't have anything to say to that. He started the car. She told him her name, and he informed her he was Paul.

"Nice to meet you, Paul." He didn't notice her outstretched hand, was too busy keeping his eyes on the street disappearing in a whorl of snow as if they were staring up a sucking vacuum hose. "Take a left at the next block. It's not far."

A couple of streets later he spoke. "What happened… between you and your husband?"

"Eventually I realized that it wasn't the way things were supposed to be. I married him when I was twenty-two. I didn't know how things were supposed to go between two people behind closed doors. My dad died when I was only five, so I never got to see him and my mom together. For all I knew, he clapped her whenever she burned his dinner or forgot to iron his shirt. Maybe that's just how it was supposed to go."

"How did you find out it wasn't?"

"It took somebody else. It always takes somebody else. My kid's elementary school teacher. Just a couple conferences, and I was filing at the courthouse. You'll never do it alone."

"I don't want to do anything."

"I'm not saying you do. It's right up here." She pointed through the tunneling snow at the brick building. Her place was just above the take-out burrito place, and in the evenings she had to keep her kitchen window open and burn incense nonstop to overpower the gristly stench of fried steak and pickled chiles. "Did you really think you were going to find a bracelet in that store that was going to make it alright?"

He pulled over to the curb, and she smelled the grease through the wind and closed windows. He held onto the wheel as if still plunging through the storm. "I don't know what you're asking. I'd never been in there, and you have some pretty stuff. I thought I might find something."

"You still might. Come up and have a drink."

"No, I don't have time. Where was that boutique you were talking about? I got to get there before they close."

She cupped a hand around his forearm, resisting the urge to examine her hand again. She tugged softly but firmly until he looked at her. "They're open as late as you need. I know the owner, and I'm a valued customer. I'll tell you what. You come upstairs, get out of the cold for a while, and I'll call down to him. He'll pick out something really nice for her, deliver it right to my door. No offense, but he knows how to pick scarves better than you."

"A scarf. That's all? That's not enough."

"I'm sure it never is, but come upstairs, and you'll see."

"No, just take me there. I don't have time—"

She let go of his arm and shoved open the door. "Find it yourself then."

He shouted after her departure, "No wait. I'll come. Just call him for me."

II

They headed up the exterior alley stairwell, the buildings on either side cutting the wind. The mist gusted up from the exhaust vent below, engulfing them in a vest of warm broth. "Sorry about the smell," she said as she unlatched the door. "Places aren't cheap around here, and to get a better one, I'd have to get something farther out and buy a car to get to work. I can't afford that."

Inside, she peeled his coat from his unwilling arms and hung it on the closet knob. He stayed against the closed door as she went into the kitchen on the other side of a half-wall of braided spindles. "Have a seat anywhere."

His choices were the royal blue velvety couch with a cushion gnarled from her long-lost cat, or one of the pair of chairs that she had gotten at an Amvets and slipcovered, dutifully tucking the loose fabric into the cracks around the cushions each time somebody stood up so the chairs looked reupholstered instead of draped in beige bed sheets. She waited for him. Where he chose to sit would answer a lot of questions.

She lit the cone of incense resting on a side table and blew it to get it going, the juniper smoke unrolling into the room, battling with the stench of a burrito supreme. "What's your drink?"

"Well...just a beer."

"Don't have one. I'm a girl living alone. You think I'm sucking on a beer bottle in the evenings? You and your honey don't frequent the cocktail bars, do you?"

"Not usually."

"Well, I'll give you something to try. It'll give you something to order from the well once in a while. Give you a

13

little class." She removed a couple of martini glasses and filled them with Grey Goose. She might've bought other people's throwaway chairs, but never would she scrimp at the liquor store. She splashed in peppermint schnapps that floated in a shimmer on top like gasoline in a rain puddle.

When she returned to the living room, he was still guarding the door. No answers. She handed him one of the glasses, and he grabbed for the bottom, then the stalk, and finally the top, taking it from her with two hands as if it were all corners, edges, and angles.

She held her glass so close to his face that he could've drunk from the other edge as she sipped from her side. She dropped the glass to her chest and leered at him until he brought his to his lips. He drank more than she did, way more than she expected, pinched his lips at the blast, but managed not to spit it back in her face. "What is it?"

"An Iceberg. Fitting, huh?" She took another drink and glanced over her glass toward the window where the snow was peppering the view of the back alley, the way a TV show looked when she was a kid, pulling in the channel from the end of rabbit ears.

"Oh shit, I got to get going." He sucked down another drink, killing over half of it, somebody looking to uncoil the springs a little. She helped him by unzipping his sweater from around his throat.

"The hell you do. I didn't make that for you to chuck and run. Be polite and finish it first." With the way he was putting it away, that might not afford her much time.

He retrieved the 3x5 picture from the built-in cubby near the door, the blonde kid waddling along the driveway inside a Little Tikes Cozy Car, hanging onto the steering wheel as if it did anything, the colors in the picture as watered out as the ancient wallpaper in her bathroom. "This your boy?"

She gulped before she spoke, letting the exhale torch up through her nostrils, hot enough to bring tears. "That's Jeremy. He got away from me in the parking lot of an IGA, started running to our car, and a pick-up truck backing up didn't see him. I hollered at him to stop, but the kid never did listen." She shrugged to let him off the hook. "His dad never listened. Why should he?"

He clung to the frame, unable to put it back before he found something decent to say, undoubtedly kicking himself that he'd touched it in the first place. She turned as he told her he was sorry. "That was too long ago." She returned her voice to the normal amplitude. "Why don't you call your honey and tell her you're still out looking? That you'll be a little late. The weather and all. Who could complain about a fella taking extra time to pick out the right present? Braving the storm. And sit down for God's sake."

She headed to the bathroom to freshen up, and set her drink on the sink. She removed her glasses, powdered her cheeks from the brass compact she had secured at an antique store a few years back, and applied another layer of burgundy lipstick to bring back the shine and fill in the winter cracks. She sucked her cheeks into sinkholes, held them there for a couple seconds to pull out the slack, and let them go. Then she pressed a finger to the sag below her eyes that she'd had since she was in her twenties, letting it drop back into place. She powdered over both sides to smooth out the textured skin, and cover up the darkness of too many long hours in that store. Her dress had started out primly enough that morning, but the flaps had separated somewhere along the line to reveal a hollow of cleavage. She left it and removed the clip from her hair, letting

15

the tangle of red curls drop to her shoulders, forking her fingers through it to take out the crimps of being clamped all day. She left her glasses on the sink, wasn't going to have to see far away tonight anyway. There. She could pass for forty, maybe 38 after his Iceberg, but the truth of it was that she could be as young as he wanted her to be.

She sidled along the short stretch of wall just outside the living room and his view of her. He was mumbling, and it took a moment for her to pick up what he was saying. "I have been…Just someone who needed a ride home…I just gave her a ride. She would've had to walk home in the storm. It's coming down out there…Inside her apartment. Right over the burrito place on Hanover. I'm leaving right now. I've got something in mind for you…Address? I don't know. Over the burrito place. I don't know what it's called. The one on Hanover. We're right upstairs. I can smell the meat from here."

Melanie burst into the room, arms splayed. He clipped his phone shut. *"Are you drinking an Iceberg or truth serum?"* The room wasn't made for such an entrance. The couch and chairs were crammed against either wall, which still allowed no more than a foot of walking room between them and the navy footlocker serving as her coffee table. She nearly cut herself off at the knees, volleyed the contents of her drink to keep it in the glass. *"What the fuck are you doing telling her where I live?* I don't need her coming over and kicking in my door."

He was sitting on the couch with his glass between his knees, the contents rattling on the surface. "She won't."

"How do you know? Why else would she want my address? I've seen some crazy ones in my time. One guy's girlfriend saw him go into the store a few times because he was so goddamn indecisive like you. She made a habit out of following him, and then she started following me. Comes

16

around here one night waving a steak knife at my front door, telling me how she's going to cut me up the center if she ever sees me with him again. She would've too. I slammed the door on her and called the cops." She pointed at the window overlooking the stairs. "Before she left, she pried a brick from the sidewalk downstairs and threw it through that window. Cops didn't catch up to her for a couple days after, but before they could, I called the guy to tell him what she did."

"You called him? How did you know his number?"

"What?"

"The guy. How did you know his number? Wasn't he just a customer?" He was paying closer attention than she suspected.

"Yeah…He gave it to me." She put her drink down on the foot locker and set to work on brushing crumbs off the edge into her cupped hands, debris from a Panini she had eaten for dinner the night before. She dumped them into an ashtray on the side table. "He was a regular, knew where to come for quality pieces, wanted me to call him if something new came in that his crazy bitch of a girlfriend might like. When I called Collin that night, he wouldn't believe it. *'Not her. Got to be somebody else. She'd never do anything like that.'* Nobody ever knows what a woman will do, especially a man. He didn't know anything."

"I know she won't come here." He hadn't sounded as sure about anything since she met him, so she let it go. "I'm going to get a present, pick up dinner and a cake someplace, and be home within an hour."

His drink was grinding down the corners of reality. The storm alone was going to delay him an hour at least, between shoveling out his car and navigating the streets that weren't going to be plowed until late that night, when the worst was over.

"How about calling that store?" he said.

She sat down with half a cushion between them. "Give me a minute to relax. I just got home." She sipped and looked straight at him; he wasn't looking back.

He finally did. "You took off your glasses," he said. He pushed his own back up on his nose.

"Give my eyes a rest." She fell against the back of the couch, and the extra foot of space between them made his features fall into a fuzz.

"Can you just call him? He might be closing up early because of the weather."

"Undoubtedly. I'm sure all the stores around here have. Nobody's out shopping in this."

"We got to get a hold of him."

She placed a hand on his back between his hunched shoulder blades, and his shoulders sank like a hydraulic jack as the air hisses out through the release valve. "A scarf isn't going to save you from her, just like a pair of earrings wasn't going to, even though our stuff is prettier than most of the real stuff. If she can't love you for getting her a present on her birthday, then there isn't anything to make her love you."

"She does love me."

"Jesus." She stood up and headed to the kitchen before he could protest. "Of course, she'll say she does, but there's no way you could really believe her." He sat watching the rest of the gasoline drain from his glass. "Or yourself when you say it." She returned with the Grey Goose but left the schnapps behind. Enough with the cocktail bars.

"I'm not sure if my ex-husband Rick started disappearing after Jeremy died or if he'd been disappearing all along. Like Jeremy in that parking lot, I never had much of a hold on him." She glanced past Paul at the picture that had vanished from that shelf in this apartment, holding no more notice for her than the porcelain owl on the shelf above it or the unburned candle on the shelf below. Was that the only picture of him in the whole apartment? Somewhere, maybe under her bed or on the top shelf of her closet, she kept a shoebox filled with all the pictures and everything else left of him.

"As soon as I took up with David, I realized how bad it had gotten. I couldn't tell until I climbed out of it for a while, saw how hopeless it was." She filled both their glasses, cradled hers and breathed down deeply, starting a fire in her lungs before drinking and starting one in her belly. She exhaled a shuddery breath. A breeze had gotten in somewhere. "He used to be Jeremy's kindergarten teacher. Jeremy wasn't around anymore when it started. Maybe because he was somebody who'd spent so much time with him, who knew him too. We could talk about him. My husband never talked about him." The snow was falling in clumps, feathers from a ripped-open pillow that you only ever saw in a gag on some stupid sitcom.

She grabbed for his hand, both of which were around his glass, but he removed one to take hers. That hand was no bigger than hers, had never wrapped around a shovel handle, screwdriver, or putty knife. Her voice steadied. "He was nice, though, and single too, not cheating on his wife or anything shitty like that. He took me to the courthouse to file, and I did, but I never moved out, just kept going on with being married until a couple weeks later when the sheriff came along with the papers I'd almost forgotten were coming. I should've been terrified. Rick had hit me for a lot less, but all he did this time was tear them up in front of my face and tell me that there was

19

absolutely nothing I could do, nothing the court could do, and nothing the boyfriend he knew I had could do to separate him from me. I knew he was right. Maybe if we still had Jeremy he could've ended up with something, but if I left, he wasn't going to have anything. Ten years and nothing to show for it."

"He's not going to come walking out of the bedroom. Is he?" Paul said. He gave a jittery laugh as if he wasn't too sure, or maybe this story had just gone on too long to keep him on schedule.

"No, he definitely won't. People come to that store thinking they're looking for some little sparkle to wrap up for their girl, and for most of them, that's what they leave with, knowing that she's going to hug them tight and show it off to her friends the next day. But there are some like you who just can't make up their cute minds." She leaned in and kissed his still lips because she was floating on Grey Goose, and who was going to stop her? He peered at her hard through smeary eyes. "They circle that store over and over like I was circling in that marriage in the end, nowhere to go and no way out. The store with all those beautiful pieces that would look good on anybody's honey; that store doesn't have what they need."

"Can you call him? He's going to close." He drained his drink and set it on the locker in front of him out of reach of the bottle.

"Relax. He lives right down the street from his store." She let go of his hand, twined her arm around his and then found that tender hand again. She leaned her cheek against the sleeve of his sweater, the wool fibers scouring the powder off as he shifted to try to face her.

"He's not going to want to go out in this, even down the street."

"Collin didn't need earrings or a scarf either for his steak knife-wielding, brick-throwing, crazy bitch of a girlfriend. I told him about my ex." She extricated her arm from his, set the bottle and her drink on the floor at her feet, and opened the footlocker she used as a coffee table, forgetting his glass was on top and sending it smashing onto the floor on the other side. Paul made a lame attempt to catch it after it was already in pieces. He stood to clean it up, but she told him, "Leave it...*Leave it*."

She dug through boxes of incense cones and random cloth napkins and scarves she had purchased from The Tailender Boutique, which actually did exist. She pulled a blue and aquamarine one out for him and slung it over his shoulder. "For your girlfriend or wife or whatever she is. The one you say would never come looking for you here, but who's probably already on her way." Her voice sounded ragged as she said it, the velvety salesgirl replaced by someone who didn't have to give a fuck. "In case I can't get ahold of my contact. But that's not what I'm looking for in here."

"It's not?" He removed the scarf from his shoulder and took a look at it. "You got a box?"

"Not even close to what I got for you."

III

S he came out with a wooden cigar box, lifted it like a container full of home-assembled explosives, not something to place a scarf into.

The sight of the box caused him to let the scarf alone and pay attention. "What is it?"

She closed the lid of the footlocker and rested the box on top, tracing the name Macanudo with her fingertip. The box came from her grandpa who smoked them for five decades, until they had to take off his bottom lip. He gave her the box during one of her visits, and for years she kept nothing more precious in it than pocket change and hair pins. "Collin had it bad with her, and even though he tried to tell me his honey wouldn't do something like that, I knew he knew she would, knew he was scared, and knew he didn't have a way out. What do you do with someone who never is going to let you go, and who being around makes you downright terrified?

"Give them a scarf? I thought I'd cook for my husband. I knew he was getting his wick dipped somewhere else, so I couldn't use that. Cooking was going to be my way of keeping the peace for a while. I was in the library, looking through the nonfiction section for a cookbook, and I found something else way in the back. Get this title: *Poisons: A Do-It-Yourself Manual.*" She reached for her glass on the floor, drained it, poured another and started in, but stopped herself. She couldn't get goofy. Not on this topic. Not with his honey hot on her way. "I think the title would've come off as a joke for most everybody whose honey is thrilled with glass bracelets or burnt meatloaf. Not me. I wasn't laughing. I was afraid to even touch it, afraid what that meant." She had flipped through it

22

but couldn't read a word while somebody might wander into the aisle with her and see what she was holding. She stuffed it into her purse, sure as hell wasn't going to check it out. "One night about a month later I made him a seven-layer lasagna, and he even asked for seconds, though one serving would've been plenty. And here I am."

"What did you do?" He tried to shake off the vodka, tried to stand up, but she was able to haul him down with one half-tug of his arm.

"This book. I still got it somewhere around here. I should return it, because I know everything inside it now, and it wouldn't be good to have someone stumble upon it. It could be back there on the shelf to help somebody else anyway. You wouldn't believe what I found inside. It had everything: toxicity, traceability, flavor, and average time to take effect."

She finally slid back the cover to the cigar box and inside were about ten or twelve jars and vials. All had labels, but with numbers—4, 7, 12—not names. She removed one and held up a vial that somebody might've used to hold a few snorts of cocaine. This one held a white powder that could've been.

"What is it?" he said. His breath was on her cheek.

Number 4. "Strychnine. It was at least. Probably no good anymore except to give you a stomach ache. It loses its chemistry after a few days, and I've had this for a long time. I don't recommend it anyway. It does the job quickly, but if they do a toxicology, they'll find it."

She picked up a larger clear glass jar with beads inside. She unscrewed the cap and poured what looked to be dead ladybug shells into her palm. "Abrin. It's a seed that you need to crush to get at the powder inside. What's good about it is it takes at least 36 hours to work. It's nice if you want to be far away when it starts to cause the shakes. By then, anything they ate or drank would be nearly through their system, dishes cleaned and in the cupboard."

"What if they go to the hospital?" He was already asking the right questions.

"Well, you got to make sure they don't. Be someplace where there isn't one nearby like the mountains or something. Some people are so pig-headed they won't go to the hospital until they keel over. This might be good for them. The hospital couldn't pump their stomach or treat them with anything anyway. You just don't want some ER doctor poking around and asking a lot of questions about what they've had to eat."

She put the container back and began to sift through the jars as if going through a box of memories. "There's a lot to think about. How am I going to administer it? How much do I give so it does the job but won't taint the flavor? How long do I want it to take? Do I want to be around to coordinate things and clean up afterwards, or be on a hunting trip in another state and hope she abides by the plan? Do I want them to suffer or go peacefully in their sleep?" She didn't bother to pour this time, but just swigged from the bottle. She handed it to him, and he did so too. She picked up another vial marked with a 1. "This was what Collin picked."

"What?" He took it from her and looked at the teaspoon of liquid inside, jiggling it to make it jump inside the glass.

"Plain old Arsenic. It doesn't taste like anything, and they can't find it unless they're looking. When the cops picked up that crazy bitch of his, he came around and got what he needed. Bailed her out the next morning with a hot cup of coffee waiting for her in the car. When they got home, he had his stuff all packed and told her he was moving out. I always recommend you be around while it goes down, maintain control of the situation. Not being around can look just as suspicious as being there.

"He knew this girl, though. The hard part was actually getting that separation, getting her to let him leave, but when she finally relented, he knew she'd drink herself stupid. I mean, getting arrested and losing the guy she loved all at once. When the fever and the aches started to come on, she would take it for a hangover or the blues, would only drink more to numb it away, and wouldn't go near a hospital. It worked out just like he thought. Two days later they found her, while he was living with his buddy starting his life over. Nobody asked him any questions he couldn't answer."

"Christ," he said. He handed her back the vial and grabbed for the vodka, cradling it close to him, crushing it against the scarf that was hanging over his shoulder, the scarf that was supposed to get him out of the doghouse. He leaned over the arm of the couch as if he were going to puke it all up, but he just huffed. "What do you do?"

"I get people out of what they couldn't otherwise ever get themselves out of."

"How many?" He hunched there, looking across the dusty hardwood, the slats dented from her heels and scratched from the cat that had bolted out the door last year and never came back.

"As many as need it, I guess. Not many at all. When I started at the store, I began to notice the occasional shopper who looked at every last item we had without choosing a thing. Obviously, they needed to look elsewhere."

"And you took them here?" He glanced around the room as if looking for any sign of the ones who'd come before.

"No. Most of those just needed an original idea that wasn't jewelry again, like tickets to a show at The Players' Ring, or an Alaskan couples' cruise." She ran her finger along the rim of the bottle, hesitated. "Some, though, were so desperate to find just the right thing that I knew they never would. You'd look at them and see they were downright terrified to make the wrong choice."

"And then…" He took a drink instead of finishing.

"And then."

"How do you know for sure? How do you know?"

"Let me ask you. Your girlfriend…your wife."

"Girlfriend."

"How long?"

It took him a moment to figure. "Eight years."

"Eight years, and you're not married yet?"

"Close once…"

She didn't ask what went wrong. He must've come to his senses and kept the ring deep in his pocket. It was amazing she hadn't badgered him into it along the way. "How many times have you tried to break up with her?"

He looked back at her, stalled in answering. "A few."

"Never takes, huh? How many times have you wished she was out of your life?" He didn't answer, so she answered for him. "A lot?"

"I guess," he said.

"When was the last time?"

He shook his head, not knowing why she would ask. His fresh haircut was a mangle of clumps and spikes like the hide of a raccoon where it received a blast of buckshot.

"Tonight?" He kept shaking his head and arching his shoulders. "While you looked in that store and tried to find something for the person who isn't going to be happy no matter what you bring home? You were shaking while you tried to decide. You're terrified, aren't you?"

"*No,*" he said, but the word was as sturdy as a piece of butcher paper you could rip to shreds to get at the meat beneath.

"Valentine's Day is less than a month away." She let that sink in—another gift to buy and no way out. "While she's out on some shopping trip, do you ever find yourself wishing she'd just never come home?" He shook his head, kept shaking it as she went on. "Not that you ever conjured a vision of her car veering into the grill of a Mack truck or anything. I'm sure you've never wanted that..." Sure. "Just that she'd never come home. For whatever reason."

He drank from the vodka bottle, even though there was nothing left to drink but runnels at the bottom. "What about you?"

"What about me?"

"What did you choose?"

She removed vial #9. "TETS. Its full name has about 30 letters. A hundred times more lethal than cyanide. They used to use it to kill rats until too many people started dying while trying to administer it. It somehow got in this restaurant's food and ended up killing about 40 people. They banned it in the 80s, but you can mail order it from China easy enough." She rotated the vial to see around the label and handed it over to him. "Doesn't taste like anything and looks enough like parmesan cheese, especially to a guy on his third gin and tonic. Sprinkle about ten milligrams between layers three and four, and he didn't know the difference."

She took a cigarette from the stale crumpled pack in her purse and lit it up. She didn't smoke more than once a month, but sometimes they tasted too good. She let her first inhale sit in her lungs before allowing it to seep out of her lips. "He didn't even make it through the nightly news. I was in the kitchen taking my time cleaning up and fussing with anything I could find. I heard him go to the bathroom, grunt a little, and return to the couch. When I came in to check on him, he looked like he was dozing, so I left him and went to bed. That's what I told the police in the morning after I wiped away something from around his mouth that didn't look right."

"And that was it?"

"That was it. A few questions, but they already knew him. They'd been out to our house more than a couple times when things got out of hand. He was a functioning drunk who hit his wife on occasion. They did some tests, but they didn't try too hard. And nobody was pushing them to look further. About him, nobody gave a fuck." She sucked down the smoke as if in salute.

"A hundred times stronger than cyanide?"

Somebody answered for Melanie, a voice coming up from the street through the wind of the storm like metal scraping over metal. *"Paul, where the hell are you? What are you doing?"*

Paul dropped the vial into his lap. He found it and shoved it back into her hand. *"Christ."* He whispered it, a kid afraid to let his parents hear him use the Lord's name in vain.

"I see your car. You're still here. I know you're still here."

"You were right. She did come. Christ."

"The crucial thing," Melanie said, placing a hand over his forearm and pressing hard, "is to always stay cool."

She closed the cigar box, placed it in the bottom of the footlocker, and closed the lid. As Paul got up and hurried to the window, Melanie slipped the scarf from over his shoulder. "I'll wrap this up for you. I think I have a pretty little bracelet

28

to put in the box with it. We do gift wrapping free of charge. I never told you because we never got that far." He was peering out between the curtains down to the street. "It takes a little longer; you have to wait for it, but it's worth it. That's what you tell her." He didn't respond. *That's what you tell her.*

He turned and nodded as Melanie taped the ends of a long flat box and the hollering went on outside. *"Paul, you get down here. I almost ran off the road coming here. I can't believe you'd go missing on my birthday."*

Melanie spoke over her from the kitchen, where she was wrapping on the narrow stretch of counter behind the spindle wall. "You go out to her, apologize, and suggest takeout from The Rosa down the street. It's an Italian place. They got cakes there too, better than the supermarket. They'll charge you an arm and a leg, but it's one-stop shopping and plenty worth it."

He nodded again, was no longer watching out the window but looking at her. She brought him the box with gold foiled paper on it. "She'll love it…at least enough." Then from underneath, she removed another box no bigger than a ring box. It too was wrapped, but in brown paper. "And something for you. Don't get the two mixed up."

"On my goddamn birthday…" It was a battle cry on the street, the fury crumbling into sobs and gasps in a volume that he couldn't possibly miss if he were in any building on the block. Oh, what he was doing to her.

Her birthday. An odd occurrence on her birthday. Might lead people to have more questions than normal. There might be a whole slew of questions from who knows how many people who cared about her. Sure, she was possessive, demanding, probably not a lot of fun to be around, but probably not a drunk, probably not someone who threatened people with steak knives or knocked her boyfriend around, just scared the shit out of him is all. Melanie should've asked more questions, got to know his honey better.

He had #9. There might have been something better for his situation. It jumped around in his hand. There was never a perfect fit, never a perfect scenario. Most of it required making it up as you went along.

She handed him his coat. He was shaking his head, couldn't close his gaping mouth, his tongue convulsing like a ticking machine part trying over and over to do what it's supposed to. "I was barely in my twenties, beaten down by him, terrified of him. I did it. 10 milligrams. All of it.

"Put it deep inside your inner pocket." She took his arm, got him moving. "Does she like wine?" He nodded. "A good bottle from Rosa's. Spend your last penny, a bottle she can't help but drink a little too much of. It's her birthday. She should celebrate, bring down the house. Sometimes people just celebrate a little too much. It happens, and it's a shame when it does."

She pushed his mouth closed, pressed down his hair only to have it flop back up, and pushed back the glasses that had fallen again. What a little boy she had here. She kissed him again, letting her tongue slip along his lips. He pressed into her this time, his mouth moving over hers, holding there until she withdrew. Probably nothing more than the gratitude of being saved.

"Pauly, please. Come back to me." Her footfalls started up the stairs.

Melanie latched onto his coat with both fists. "Now— it's her birthday, and you're thrilled. Got her present and ready to celebrate. Glad to be hers. That's the face you give her, and that face starts it all."

He turned to the door and turned back. "Wait, I didn't pay you yet. How much?"

"The little box is on the house, just something for a friend in need. The scarf and bracelet, though. They belong to me. I want them back when you're finished with them."

"But...okay," Breathing again. "Okay, sure thing."

"See you then." She opened the door for him, letting in a whish of storm. She watched him descend the stairs to where his honey was waiting two steps up. Melanie retrieved her glasses from the bathroom and returned to the window. His honey was nothing more than a short little waif as white and wicked and ugly as the snow in the gutters.

She said something, but his voice bellowed above hers and the thrashing wind, his arms stretched out wide. *"Happy Birthday, Honey."* And that was the start of it all.

Are You Happy Here?

Lane 13 was a bunker of cigarettes, walled in six feet high on three sides with towers of Marlboro red hard packs, Kool green soft packs, orange Paradise cartons, and blue Alpine Ultra Filters. If one of those summer tornados ever decided to roll over this particular IGA, transforming the massive front windows into a fusillade, turning the cans of soup into projectiles, and raining the roof onto everybody inside, Jessica, in Lane 13, with her curling-ironed brunette hair, smile as flat and dead as a desert horizon, and five years of loyal service, would likely end up being the one and only survivor.

Nick began setting his groceries on the static conveyor belt as Jessica ran the five packs of Newport Menthol Kings over the scanner one by one for the woman in front of him who had a matted head of hair the texture of an air conditioning filter, and cheeks like ground beef gone gray from too long a stay in the butcher's case. She declined a bag and clamped the packs in her caramel-stained knuckles, would undoubtedly fish one out for her long, cold walk to the car. Left behind in the lane just ahead of Nick was a pocket of the scorched atmosphere in which she existed, the same one that had trapped him all through school, puffing from the pores of his clothes, packaging him like a dense woolen sweater as he moved along his day, and eliciting a crinkled expression from any kid who sat nearby and didn't have a mom who laid out his clothes, poured his bowl of Kix, and drove him to school, all with a Salem clipped between her fingers.

"How could there be so many smokers in the world?" Nick asked. Hadn't most of the older generation like that woman and his ma, who hadn't known any better before all the studies and stamped on warnings, died premature deaths, or at least traded in the cigarette for an oxygen tube? Hadn't the younger generation realized yet that starting up this particular habit relegated them to an ashen, wrinkled existence on the sidewalks and back alleys of the world for passersby to wonder why they didn't just stop poisoning the air for everybody else and use a gun or pills if they wanted to kill themselves so badly?

"Once it gets its hooks into you," Jessica said. She knew what she was talking about, would certainly be taking her break out in the back alley with her death of choice, but as of yet, you couldn't see the decay on her. The girl was just like the other kids working the registers, who would all live forever and were just passing through on their way to somewhere else: college, the military, or some union job on an assembly line that would provide for a two-kid family, but not three. She began to run his groceries, blindly reaching for any container in her grasp, waiting for the beep, exchanging hands, and then pushing whatever it was into the bagging trough. She stayed focused on the keyboard in front of her, though there was nothing to key in.

It was then Nick noticed the neon pink laminated sign taped over the register which ludicrously read: **I am happy here.** He just had to ask her: "Are you happy here?"

She glanced up to see who was asking, huffed a laugh, and proceeded to scan his bag of Eight O'clock coffee. She'd obviously been asked before by other clever customers, and this response had always sufficed in getting them to mind their own business. With Nick, it didn't. "Are you?"

33

"If they have to hang up a sign proclaiming it, then you probably know the answer."

"Is it a reminder or an order?"

"My manager hung it up. Ask him."

Somewhere out in the parking lot, a car alarm started shrieking, freezing Jessica's hand as it reached for his carton of half and half. She resumed her mechanical movements, but Nick stared at her, waiting for something. Eventually she asked, "Are *you* happy?" Her question was like a switchblade she was waving around to get him to back off. *Take a look at your own life before you examine mine.*

Maybe he'd been wanting for her to turn the question back around to him. "Actually, I am. You didn't happen to vote 'yes' on question 1, did you?" He didn't let her answer. She probably didn't even know what question 1 was, might not even know there was an election last week with three questions at the bottom of the ballot, the first of which meant a whole lot more to him than even who ended up becoming president. "Well, it passed, and I…" He pulled the box from his jacket, opened it up to reveal a white gold band studded with chips of diamonds that weren't going to pop the eyes out of anybody's head, but were big enough to spray a little sparkle around if the light hit them just right. "I've been saving for it since I learned about the referendum. I wasn't even sure if you're supposed to get a ring. I had to go online and ask the experts. They said sometimes yes, sometimes no, but I just wanted to get something for him, couldn't ask empty handed. He needs to know it means something."

Jessica showed no pause of realization and the subsequent sputtering Nick dreaded seeing in people right when it occurred to them, had dreaded it since coming out right after graduating high school, although gradually dreading

34

it less and less as the years passed by. She just glanced to make sure nobody was behind him and observed the ring, her mouth staying flat and closed. No reaction could shake him more than his mother's ten years before, as she lay in the hospice, nothing more to do about the spot discovered on her lung after six months of trying, except to flood her brain with morphine and wait for her body to give up. No more could she curse his father for running out on them before raising his boy not to be such a goddamn crybaby, or sign Nick up for summer baseball because a boy just had to play something, or invite Mattie from down the block over for a surprise lunch because she was so pretty and such a darling and perfect for him if he'd only give her a chance. It was finally safe to tell his mother what she'd known all along. He hadn't been able to see her expression change behind the oxygen mask, but she rolled her head to stare at the paint-by-number portrait of a tugboat hanging on the wall, ending his confession and his visit right there. He knew that everything just had to be easier from that moment after.

"I'm going to make him a nice dinner at home, and get a fire going," Nick told Jessica. "And afterward, I'm going to do it. I figure six years is enough time together." Six years since Phil had been absolutely heartless from behind the ER counter the first time they met, Nick mashing a blood-sodden handkerchief against his forehead while being told that he needed to return to the waiting area and fill out the clipboard of forms before the doctor could take a look at his busted open skull. Two hours later, though, Phil appeared in the examining room to check on Nick, though it wasn't his job, and brought with him a plate of chicken parmesan from the cafeteria along with an apology because by the time Nick had come in, it had already been some long night. He brushed Nick's hair away to get a look at the sixteen stitches curving across his forehead, winced, and then sat down as if having all the time in the world to listen to what happened.

Jessica held up the Styrofoam package. "You're making dinner to pop the question, and you get reduced ribeye, instant mashed potatoes, and canned beans? Better ask him first before you serve him up this, or you won't get the answer you're looking for. Isn't cooking supposed to be one of your things?"

Nick snapped the box closed and returned it to his pocket. "Along with interior decorating and dog grooming. I'm on a budget. Phil usually does the cooking, and he'll appreciate it that I did."

"He'll appreciate it? That steak's probably been hosed off and relabeled at least three times already." She scanned it anyway and resumed focusing on her keypad. "I'm sure he'll like it fine."

Nick gripped the box in his pocket hard enough to feel the metal shell within the velvet skin dimple and pop out. Phil would like it fine. He would be thrilled, and together they could face the rest of the world and all the barbs that came along with it, including petulant cashiers who didn't have anything good to say about anything, or shit kicking cowboys who liked to show their friends how fun it was to bounce faggots off brick walls.

Nick nodded toward the sticker on her nametag as she punched in the code for Macintosh apples—what would become his dessert of apple crisp—and set the four of them on the scale. "Five years. That's quite a stint."

"Seven now," she said. He had once again become any other customer for whom she needed to make the obligatory small talk until he rolled his cart away past the rack of gumball machines, out the door, and out of her life forever.

"This place must have something."

"Something?"

"Yeah, something worthwhile that made you stick around for so long."

She locked onto him suddenly, her left hand in a death grip around one of his apples. "Something. Seven years ago, I got this job to save money for college and buy my neighbor's Volkswagen. Then I didn't have any parents anymore, and things changed."

"What?" Nick latched onto the edge of the conveyor and asked the question before he could stop himself. "What happened?"

"Our furnace backed up and poisoned my mom and dad while they were sleeping. Same thing would've happened to me and my brother if we weren't sleeping upstairs. Another hour…"

"I'm sorry," Nick said, but she rolled over him.

"He was just twelve then, and if I didn't take care of him, nobody would've. So I picked up more hours here and never got the Volkswagen."

He didn't inquire about college. "How's he doing now?"

"He just finished his first year at UMA. Civil engineering major. You believe that? Going to design bridges. My little brother." She showed her first smile, holding it as she gazed out the picture windows at the pipsqueak kid shoving his shoulder into the line of carts he'd collected from the lot, skittering them across the pavement.

"Then you did your job," Nick said.

It brought her back to him. "Yeah, I guess I did."

"So now you work here to pay for his college?"

"No, the scholarships pay for most of that. You'd be surprised how many people will give you money if you're young and on your own. Anything else he needs, the insurance money pays for." She hit the total button but didn't tell him the damage.

"So what are you saving for now?"

"Thirty-five sixty-eight."

He didn't reach for his wallet. He returned to the neon sign over the register. For maybe one moment in your life, you can say that you are, can say that absolutely nothing is wrong, that everything is ideal, and that nothing could change to make your life any better than it is right now, and when you reach that moment, you want that for everybody, can't bear to let anybody go on living without. "They'd give money to you too."

"Who?"

"Those people who gave it to your brother."

"To do what?" she said. Her bagger had jumped to Lane 12 to bag for the woman with the baby balanced on her hip, two more kids at her knees, and two tons of groceries to feed them for the week. Jessica had to bag for herself, burrowing a hand into the plastic bag to poof it out.

"Something," he said. He'd just been promoted from copy editor to freelance editor. It wasn't much more than a change in title, but it proved that if you worked for it, you could go places. "Something more than coupons and cigarettes. You had plans once. You could make bridges too, could make anything. What were you saving to do?"

She dropped an apple into the bag, bouncing it off the metal underneath. "What?"

"At college?"

She held back the answer for a moment, but eventually it came, her voice dropping as if an afterthought. "I never decided. Maybe journalism. I used to write articles for the high school paper. I liked that."

"Then do it," he said. "Your brother did."

She grabbed his bottle of Barefoot chardonnay. "Jesus, do you need help. Are you serious? He's going to wake up tomorrow with a jackhammer in his head. Do you want him to forever associate your proposal with being sick as a dog?"

A guy filed in behind Nick with a twelve pack of Olympia and two bags of Doritos, ready for a night of entertaining, but she barricaded his approach by placing a **Closed, Next register please** tent on the conveyor. He opened his mouth to protest, but she flipped on the blinking light above her register, letting him know it was a lost cause.

"What's wrong?" Nick said. She didn't reply. He'd overstepped. It wasn't his business. This was his moment, not hers. Maybe her moment had already passed, or maybe it was a long way off, or maybe, with or without his input, it would never arrive at all. Before he could apologize, some scrawny guy in a clip-on polyester tie came over. He looked younger than she was.

"What's up?" he said.

"Can you void out this order and have somebody put all this stuff back? He doesn't want it." The guy, whose name tag read **Brian - Crew Chief,** opened his mouth to ask why not, but she spoke before he could. "Because it's all wrong. None of it's right. Somebody will have to cover for me too. I'm going home."

Again he opened his mouth to ask why, but again was beaten to it. "Because I feel sick. I feel like I'm going to puke. Do you want me to puke all over somebody's porkchop?" He didn't argue. She removed her apron, threw it on the conveyor, and came out from her cigarette fortress, burrowing a hand in the front pocket of her diarrhea-colored pants.

Nick stalled there with nothing to show for his fifty minutes of combing the aisles and watched her as she produced a soft pack from her pocket. She plucked out a cigarette and rapped the filter three times against the corner of her hand. "You want to really do it right? Then go back and start over." She chopped a look at him like she must've done to her brother while she was still in charge of his world, but now he was pushing back because she wasn't his mother.

Nick didn't move from the lane, just gaped at her, would undoubtedly return to the same boxed food aisle and the same discount meat cooler, because that was how his mother had always done it.

Jessica headed out of the aisle toward the 'Out' door, swinging closed after someone's departure, but she paused next to the carriage corral behind the row of baggers and placed the cigarette in her mouth. Producing a Bic from her pocket, she lit up the cigarette right there in the store and inhaled impossibly long and impossibly deep like someone at the bottom of a swimming pool trying to break her friend's record staying underwater and willing to burst her lungs doing it. The whole store—cashiers sliding through barcodes, baggers brutalizing fruit, a woman tugging her kid to come on away from the candy rack, Brian turning his manager key in the register to void Nick's order without knowing why, but too scared to inquire again—all ceased their movements at once to wonder at her. She exhaled upward into space to spare them so much smoke that formed a Jupiter over her, rising toward the high ceiling.

Brian broke out of his trance just then and started saying her name "Jessica…Jessica," issuing a universal, "Sorry folks," to anybody who'd listen while telling her that she couldn't do that in here, needed to take that outside. As if she didn't know the rules after seven years of devoted service. Brian was probably hustling her out by the arm while asking her what she thought she was doing and informing her, in case she was wondering, that yes, she was indeed fired…if a crew chief even had that authority. The shoppers must've all been watching the events unfold with grateful amazement at having the slightest diversion from their daily tedium, mothers undoubtedly covering their children's mouths as if one whiff of second-hand smoke was going to produce spots on their tiny lungs when most of those mothers had survived growing up in a house like Nick's where the only choice was to breathe it in every single day of their lives.

Nick didn't know for sure what was happening around him, though. He was looking upward at the last hazy remnants of her exhale compressed against the ceiling, unrolling outward across the foam tiles to the four corners, and sucking up and away and gone between the greasy slats of the circulation vent.

A Hard Bet

Mary rose from sheets so sopping with sweat they felt like rained-on garbage bags wrapped around her. His voice came across the room out of the sweat and dingy morning shadows. "You know, you make one shitty T-Bone."

She hurled the top sheet from around her, the straight jacket removed, sending it into a clump on the floor. The only light in the room came from behind him, a bubble-shaped screen showing an animated sardine sashaying down the road with an Empire top hat on, and a fat cigar between his fish lips. Somebody needed to play with the vertical hold on the TV, which must've been purchased sometime around when Ford was president, because the picture only held for a second before flipping upward, holding and flipping again, the motion adding to the roiling of her stomach and the flopping between her temples.

She didn't know this TV, didn't know the chunky carpet under her feet, and didn't know the mattress she had just woken on, balanced on milk crates probably stolen from behind some convenience store. She could just remember that T-Bone and him making her wait while he rolled the first bite over in his mouth to make sure it was edible, exposing a collection of steel-blue molars that looked like he'd just been chewing up bullets. That moment was the last she could remember, from there to here just a long black road. "I didn't make it. I just served it."

She was still wearing the navy blue waitress uniform from her shift the night before at The Broken Plate, the polyester sliding greasily over her thighs with the same texture as one of the Alaska-sized pork tenderloins fresh out of the fryer still shiny with liquefied lard, served for seven bucks to fish who'd been emptied out at the sawdust card houses two blocks over, but had the sense to forgo one last hopeless bet for one last meal, except rarely budgeting in any money for a tip or even managing not to be an asshole to the person serving them for free. Last night she had delivered a T-Bone to a guy who had sent it back twice because both times it had failed to spurt blood onto the plate when he cut into it. The last steak she served surely had been basted with snot snurgled up from the back of the cook Carl's throat before he waved the raw meat over the grill, called it done, and warned Mary not to come back again. The guy at the table with the wraparound buzz cut, shag of hair up top, and tunnels burrowed through his earlobes finally accepted it, and his girl sitting next to him, somebody who'd probably never sent a meal back in her life, finally let the tightness fall out of her cheeks.

"Maybe you should've cooked it. Couldn't do any worse." She couldn't see his ratty face in the shadows, but she remembered it well enough.

"What happened to your girl?" She might've asked him something more pressing, but she didn't want to let him know how many questions she had no answer to.

"What happens to every girl? She hangs on you for a little while, for a free meal or two, a few laughs, until she finds something better coming her way."

She began to feel through the bedding for her purse, keeping the conversation going, but not so it sounded like she gave a goddamn. "Better than you? Seems unlikely."

The ember of his cigarette showed through the darkness every minute or so. "Maybe she felt too much competition. I never thought in a million years you'd accept my invitation to join us for a nightcap. But then you did, and she knew she didn't stand a chance."

"Probably crying in her pillow right now." She only half said it, and it didn't slow him down.

"You got something she'll never have—no fear. You ain't like any of the rest of them at all, terrified to eat with their mouths open or walk into a room first." The cigarette blazed as he considered her. "Something happened to you that made you not care, something seriously bad, I got to think, makes you willing to walk into the fire."

"You don't make a lick of sense." She could suddenly remember settling up for the night, and him still being there in her section as she went to wipe down her tables, his gal still beside him but eyes on the door. She asked a question before he could explain what he meant. Who knows what she told him last night? "Why didn't you take me home at least to change?" It was a dangerous question because he might go into detail about what happened here in the dark, but asking it was a place to start. Start there and work forward or backwards, depending on which direction this answer took her. She could've walked home from the diner and changed out of this polyester waitress rag, couldn't imagine that she didn't insist on it if she was planning to go out after her shift.

"Oh girl, that was the last place you wanted to go. After serving lowlifes all night—present company included—you needed to cut loose, and needed some help doing it."

"Your help?" She didn't think he heard her ask.

"That's why you were so good to me in the first place. Most gals throw me out after the second steak. I've never been served a third. I knew you were some kind of special. Damaged, sure, but special nonetheless."

"Damaged," she said, shaking her head to let him know he was full of shit. The clank in her head was a crowbar being repeatedly dropped onto concrete, metal on stone, over and over again. And where was the door out of this place? Her eyes were beginning to adjust to the darkness. The morning light streamed in through the crack at the edge of the drawn curtains, illuminating the doorway out of the bedroom. She sidled toward it, but kept her eyes on him, wanted his recitation of last night to end there. She tugged down on her dress, though it was down as far as it would go, and he couldn't see her boney knees in the dark anyway.

"You ain't easy, that's for sure. Raked me over for a good half hour as if I'd wrapped a chain around your throat and dragged you to that bar stool to drink that tequila. But you loosened up real good after you got a couple in you. Some kind of thirsty, you were."

The walls were so thin in this place she heard a baby whining awake which promptly gave way to wailing. The crib must've been right on the other side of his wood-paneled bedroom wall. She moved away from that sound. "How close am I to a bus stop?"

"Where do you think a bus is going to take you?"

"Home, unless I'm close enough to walk." She hoped this required a bus ride, didn't like the idea of him living within walking distance of her place.

"You have arrived."

"What?"

"You are home."

She headed for the doorway. "That's very nice. Can I just have a glass of water before I split? My head..." She couldn't think of a way to describe it, just knew she would dissolve into dust on the bumpy bus seat if she didn't get a drink first. Her face felt like donut glaze.

"Go ahead. It's your water too. We go halves on everything now."

The crying wasn't helping either. Somebody needed to wake up and pick that baby up, but nobody was. The sound made her rush out of the room, finding a kitchen no bigger than the inside of a Civic, light coming in through a window overlooking a stream of trash and sewage. She filled a crusty glass from his cabinet, gulping down the water and hunks of dust. He came up behind her. "Somebody needs to tend to that baby," she said.

"Not likely. They're probably all cranked up, will let that kid scream night and day while they take that ride. Meanwhile, the rest of us have to listen to it. He's not long for this world." His breath was all cigarette smoke and broth, shreds of last night's steak probably still jammed between his teeth and rotting there slowly.

"How could they? We need to…" She didn't finish, brushed past him without looking back, didn't want to see him in the light. "I have to go home." She headed into the living room of discarded take-out wrappers and Goodwill furniture. He didn't follow. Right there on the coffee table was a black bound book that stalled her. She picked it up and trailed her fingers across the flaky gold letters stamped into the furry leather. *The New Jerusalem Bible.*

She transported it to the front door, but finally discarded it on the arm of a chair as she turned the knob. As the light severed the darkness, he called out behind her, "That's going to be a mighty long trip."

She stepped out onto the second-floor concrete walkway overlooking the streets, a line of apartment doors

46

running in either direction. She expected to see somewhere out there the strip twinkling through the morning. No matter where she drove in the city, she could never get fully away from it, even if it was just a glow rising up from the horizon to attract all the world's bugs to the flame. The only light she saw now, though, was a rotating Texaco sign across the street offering $3.79 for unleaded. Beyond the station was a road of filthy-looking, one-room businesses: convenience stores, laundromats, doughnut shops, all providing for all the nearby clapboard apartment complexes as crappy as this one. The world out there was too flat and grim to be hers.

She wanted to ask how the hell she'd gotten here, but she already knew the answer: her mother dying of lung cancer before Mary knew her, and her dad dead in a car accident when Mary was in seventh grade, leaving her in the care of Grandnan, who was just too old to make her do her homework or keep her grounded after she was caught smoking a joint in the school bathroom, or make her care about anything beyond who was having a party next weekend because all Mary had left was an old lady who wasn't going to be around long and was going to leave her to a future all alone. Then there was Charlie, who straightened her out enough that she squeaked through to graduation, so into his church that their weekends consisted of the two of them going door-to-door and sharing the word, saving the ones who didn't slam the door in their faces, saving the world and saving Mary in the process, until, that is, she missed a month and he rewrote the history between them for his church and parents, claiming that they had never been anything more than friends, certainly never laid down together, but whoever was the true culprit, Charlie would certainly pray for both their souls. She was left to raise Eric on her own with the help of Grandnan, who ended up being around after all and would watch him in the day when Mary worked a temp job filing patient sheets in Dr. Garrison's office and in the evenings when she started taking nursing classes. Five classes away from graduating with an LPN degree when Eric got leukemia and died four months later. Only five classes, but what was the point anymore? The only thing to do was drive away from everything to someplace else entirely, and where better than a place with so many lights to wash away the darkness, and so many people with so many sins and so much pain worse than hers.

He answered the question she'd never asked, "You got to be careful. A few too many tequilas and you might just let somebody drive you 200 miles from where you started. You might have to leave it all behind and start over from there."

She came back inside and turned away from the door to face him, his lips white and fractured from being as dried out as she was. His complexion was all pocked and pimply and prickly. She found the wall, the door shutting to a sliver. She liked him better wrapped up in shadows.

He went on. "That place you came from would suck out your soul sooner or later. Girl on her own has to take a big gamble if she wants to survive. It's called a hard bet." He brought a hand up to her face, every finger including his thumb wearing a spikey pewter ring that with a backhand could rip somebody's cheek apart. "I told you there weren't two ways about it, that if you decided to come with me, meant you were mine. And here you are. Now shut the door, and let's have our breakfast. I like steak with my eggs."

She knew he did. His hand left her face, and she could've made a dash for the street, might've made it too. She knew how to run.

Instead she fell back into the apartment, where inside the fridge she found them freshly wrapped in butcher paper and tied with white twine, not one but two, as if he expected her, or somebody, or anybody, but here she was. She set them on the counter, cut the twine to let the paper relax from around them, and went about looking for a frying pan.

Circus World

I

Keisha is just about to lower the cage over the storefront of Claire's Boutique upstairs when the blonde out in the mall says, "Hey, what's that store down there?" She's pointing down to the lower level and leaning so far over the railing that her gangly body might tip ass-over-teakettle and send her plummeting into the coin fountain below. "It used to be a toy store. Remember?" She is asking her husky, dark-haired friend who's leaning against the planter, wearing a jean skirt she should've rethought.

Her friend shrugs.

You have to put a key in the wall to lower the cage, and with ten minutes to go until closing, Keisha planned to lower it a quarter of the way to give the few stragglers the hint. She holds off, though, to get a load of these two crazy-ass Beckys out there.

"Come on, they had a clown out front and balloons. The sign's dark. I can't read it from here. What was it called? I used to take Tommy there all the time, whether I wanted to or not. He'd go berserk about going in every time we walked past it. I can't believe it's closed. When did that happen?" She stands back up from the railing. Got to be topping six feet, this one. Usually, Keisha wouldn't have been able to hear her, even shouting as she is, among the din of so many other conversations going on at White Oaks Mall, but these two are

50

about the only ones around this time of night, and the blonde might as well have had a microphone on stage. Her craggy voice is all you can hear up and down this upper leg. "God, I haven't been to this mall in so long."

"Come on, Peggy, let's find something and go," her friend says.

Just then a couple of kids come into view, a freckly girl no older than thirteen, the kind of girl who tumbles into Claire's shouting and laughing with a riot of friends clinging to each other and about five bucks to spend between them. She is only with her brother now, though, holding his hand. The blonde latches onto her arm.

"Hey, you remember the toy store down there? What was it called?" The freckly girl has no answer for her, which causes Peggy to take a look at who she's talking to and go a little apeshit. "What the hell are you two doing out by yourselves so late?" She has to stoop over, nearly fall over, to get into her face. "This time of night. With your little brother in tow. Are you stupid?"

"It's only nine o'clock."

"You see him?" the blonde asks them. She points over the girl's shoulder beyond where Keisha can see down to the end cap that used to be Sears before it went out of business and is now a dark hole behind its permanently descended cage, no other department store dumb enough to take its place when the world is moving away from indoor malls. "What do you think he's doing there?" The girl can do nothing but push the glasses up onto her nose. "He's waiting for you and your brother. That's what. Going to put you in his car and take you nowhere you'd ever want to go. Then nobody will see neither of you ever again. How would you like that?" Again, the girl doesn't seem to have an answer.

51

"Come on, Peggy," her friend says. Peggy releases her grip, and the freckly girl and her brother hustle away. "Jesus, Peggy," her friend says.

Peggy studies their departure toward the exit doors around the corner from Sears. *"Right home,"* she hollers after. Her voice has a tunneling effect traveling down the length of the mall. Then her focus shifts slightly, and she calls out to whomever she warned them about. *"And you. You stay the fuck away from them. You hear me? I see what you look like. I know who you are."*

"Is everything okay?" some guy says from somewhere else Keisha can't see, probably a minimum wage security guard armed with a walkie talkie, a whistle, and a ham sandwich.

"No, it's not okay. It's a far shit from okay. You see them?" Peggy points without looking at him. "Those two sweet little things. Make sure they get to their car, okay? Go." He appears in his baby blue uniform and heads down toward Sears. He's on the case.

"Come on, Peggy," her friend says. "He's nobody."

"Sure."

Keisha turns the key, and the cage descends from the ceiling. She's seen enough of the kooks tonight, so she decides to take it all the way down ten minutes early. Half the stores around her have closed already, because with this traffic, why bother? She has to get cooking on counting the deposit anyway. Too much cash in the drawer.

The hum of the motor catches Peggy's friend's attention, who tugs Peggy to hurry. She calls across the space for Keisha to hold up; they have to buy something.

"Oh, hell no," Keisha says, but the chick says again that they need to buy something. Keisha releases the key, and the gate stalls halfway down. She'll get these white bitches in and out, and any other stragglers will see the cage and get the hint.

"Do you believe that shit?" Peggy is saying as they come this way. "Hanging around this place with that little boy when things are closing down and nobody else around."

Keisha returns to her place behind the counter, overlooking rows of inventory occupying the tiny triangle of space wedged between Hot Topic and The Limited, the walls and floors crammed with so much cheap shit: unicorn purses, tin charm bracelets, rainbow scarves, watermelon headbands, starburst backpacks, polar bear change pouches. The place looks like the living room of some ancient grandma who in fifty years hasn't thrown away one newspaper, twist tie, or paperclip, and the poor family will need to hire an earth mover to clear the place out when she finally kicks it.

The two come inside, the shorter one only having to duck a little, but Peggy, the blonde beanpole, having to nearly get on her knees. "Why the hell do you have this down?"

"It's closing time," Keisha says.

"According to that clock, it ain't," the friend says. "We got ten minutes."

"Close to closing time."

"I'm going to lose my head on this thing."

"What was that all about?" Keisha asks them. She takes out a rag and wipes the counter free of the Cinnabon fingerprints that two tweenagers left while standing at the counter, picking at the goopy thing between them, and waiting for Keisha to ring up their junk.

"My little Tommy," Peggy says as she stands up. "And a couple of stupid shits back there." She removes a prescription bottle from the white vinyl purse that hangs from a chain over her exposed shoulder, and she mashes her palm against the top to uncap it. She was due for another bathtub rinse job about three weeks ago, her roots seeping up from the part cut down the center of her head like silt floating up from a clogged drain.

Keisha has no idea what she means, but doesn't ask her to explain.

"Hey, share one of those," her friend says.

"Fine, you grub." Peggy hands her one of the pills, and returns the cap to the bottle. "Yo, Gina, give me some of that." She's referring to the strawberry Big Slug Slushie that her friend is faithfully slurping on, the cup so wide she can barely get her hammy fingers around it, even with two-inch long, epoxied-on blue nails. There's a sign posted near the door prohibiting food or drink inside, but if either of them sees it, they don't give two shits. Peggy pops the pill and drinks it down, her lips pruning as she swallows. "Jesus, this thing is going to fill up your ass like a pan full of brownies." She hands it back to her friend. "I wouldn't drink that many calories even if it was floating on a sea of rum."

"It's so good, though. It tastes like…" Gina can't come up with what exactly before occupying herself with the straw again. The Volkswagen-sized ass underneath her raggedy denim skirt tells Keisha this is not the first strawberry Big Slug she's sucked down in her life. Gina veers from her friend to observe the license plate purses hanging on the mirrored wall. She opens one with her free hand and roots inside as if out might pop a roll of Benjis or a forgotten J for the taking. "How about one of these, Peggy?" They must've been at it for a while. "Let's buy it and get the hell out of here."

Peggy wears bleach-splatter jeans with self-inflicted tears through the denim, and a tangerine top with a gaping neckline hanging lazily off one bra-strapped shoulder down to the crook of her elbow, as if the shirt inadvertently fell and she hasn't gotten around to hauling it up again. She's like so many other moms Keisha has seen coming in here with cut-out shoulders because their shoulders are the only place on them that hasn't begun to hangdog. "No, not a purse. She doesn't have anything to put in it. Too young to have a job and make her own money, but I can't wait until she does and actually has a reason to leave the house."

"How about make-up then? She needs something on those fish lips."

"Jack doesn't let her wear none. Not until she's fifteen, he says, but I know the little sneak is laying it on as soon as she leaves the house each morning. Probably walks the halls looking like some back alley whore." Peggy there must've spent the whole of last summer lying around in the sun, but in November, her copper color has faded to that of butterscotch pudding. Cocoons hang beneath her eyes, and the skin around her mouth has developed cracks like the concrete of an old driveway poured into place decades ago, and gradually broken up by the cold and the rain and so many years of being walked upon.

"Can I help you find something?" Keisha asks from behind the counter.

Peggy looks up from the perfume bottle whose pink atomizer she has just squeezed, and horrors at the fragrance Keisha knows is labeled as 'cherry blossom', but smells more like mosquito repellent. "Are we keeping you from something, girl?"

"It's just that we close in five minutes," she says.

"But you ain't closed now?" Peggy says.

"No, we ain't closed now, but in five minutes—"

"But you ain't closed now?"

55

"No, we ain't closed now." Her mouth closes, and her lips squinch as if she is signaling to a boy that she is ready to be kissed for the very first time but doesn't know when it's coming, her molars aching as top and bottom crush down on each other. She hits the no sale on the register, and she stops the springing open drawer with her hip, revealing the row of coin troughs in the front without showing the bills busting out of the slots behind. Bridget, the woman who owns the franchise with her husband and manages days while he maintains his job as an insurance adjuster, went heavy on the cocktails last night at some friend's bachelorette party. She barely made it in today and dragged herself out of here as soon as Keisha showed up at four, without even doing her afternoon cash out. Now Keisha has about three times what she usually has to count, but she'll have to wait on that until there aren't two pill-popping dimwits in the store.

"Good," Peggy says. "Because I got to find something for my boyfriend's daughter. It's her birthday tomorrow, and you're the only game in town."

Gina flutters her fingers through the feathers of a wind catcher hanging along the wall. "About everybody else has closed up early. Ain't there some kind of rule they can't close up before nine?"

"Not on Saturday night when people got something better to do than come to the mall. How about a locket?" They happen to be right in front of Peggy. Her friend separates from her straw to repeat Keisha's question.

Peggy lifts one of the cardboard backings from the turnstile and examines it. She has glued-on nails too, two-inch red ones, but at least two of them have fallen off, leaving her with pink stubs that look so hideous against the rest that they might've been the result of her reaching down into a stalled

56

blender of margaritas to dislodge an ice cube. Her middle fingernail has a rhinestone glued to it, which Keisha imagines must provide an exclamation point whenever Peggy finger-bombs the next person who comments on her roots.

She releases the locket. "No, then I got to figure out whose picture to put in it. Trisha hates her daddy, and she hates me more, and no way am I putting in the dog ass picture of her baby mama."

"How old is she going to be?" Keisha focuses on the fistful of quarters that she nudges back into the drawer one by one with her thumb. Bridget lives only a mile away from White Oaks, and maybe after sleeping off her brown-bottle flu, she might feel obligated to pop in and help Keisha with such a big deposit. Not if Keisha gets it done first, though.

"Thirteen. Ain't that a bitch?" Peggy takes out a compact and smooths down one of the false lashes that have begun to unpeel from her lower lid. "I used to change her diapers. Now I'm down to five more years." It isn't clear who she's telling. "And as soon as she turns eighteen, she is out of the house. I'll even pack up all her shit for her and deposit it onto the curb. And Jack better not have one goddamn word to say about it—I swear to God. I done my time with that brat. I done enough." She dabs at her red sticky lips and then claps the compact closed.

"Pick something out," her friend says, slurping again, too much taste registering in her face. "Pick anything. Why are you trying so hard?"

"Shut up, Gina."

"I want to go to Ruby Tuesdays. I want a Rum Runner. It's my night out for God's sake. I paid for a sitter and everything. And not to spend all night at the mall." She arbitrarily pulls back the end ball of a Newton's cradle on the glass shelf in front of her and watches the balls clack from one end to the other and back again.

"She doesn't like anything. That's the problem. None of this crap."

Keisha feels obligated to defend Claire's, but all she can say is, "The mood rings aren't half bad." She drops the last of the quarters in the slot, writes $8.75 on the slip of paper. "See, I have one." Keisha holds her hand out so that Peggy can see it on her finger. "They really work too. Show blue if you're in a great mood and then green when things go a little sour on you like someone says something nasty, and brown if you're just in a funk and black if it's just one of those days when you can't bring yourself to do anything but hate the world."

Peggy takes one from a display rod and runs her finger along the silver frame without touching the glass orb, as if afraid that it might reveal something about her she doesn't want the world to know. "How the hell does it do that?"

"It's not really your mood. It's your temperature that changes it. Put it in a freezer, it goes black, or rub it with your thumb and it goes blue."

"What a fake-out," Peggy says. She puts it back.

Gina has stopped drinking her slushie with about half left, the straw and inside of the cup coated in a strawberry scum. "Just get it. She won't know the difference."

"It's going on nine now," Keisha says.

"What's your hurry, girl?" Peggy says.

"Don't you be calling me that." She stalls fifteen dimes in.

"Don't be calling you what?"

"Don't call me that." This bitch knows.

"Hey, she don't mean nothing by it," Gina says. She comes over like a peacekeeper. She's wearing a washed-out

58

Black Sabbath concert shirt, the black gone to gray, with a devil baby on the front and a 1987 tour name 'Born Again' on the back. The hem of the jean skirt hangs in dregs over cobbly thighs and knees like garlic knots. "She calls everybody that. She calls me girl. She calls Trisha girl…" She runs out of examples. "That's what she calls everybody."

"Not me," Keisha says. "She doesn't call me that."

"Fine, what do I call you then?" Peggy says. She pulls out a crumpled pack of Kools from her purse, a miniature Bic lighter tucked in the tattered cellophane casing. She removes a cigarette that looks like it's been run over by a truck, and lights it right there in the store.

"Keisha, and you can't smoke in here."

Peggy blows her exhale to the ceiling. "Chill out, Keisha, your manager isn't here this late, is he? You want one?"

Sure, she does, has three Cats waiting in her purse that she copped from her mom's pack on her way out of the house, is jonesing for one right about now, but if Bridget comes in and sees her smoking, sees this one smoking… At least Keisha can tell Bridget she told her not to. "I'm the manager, and you can't smoke in here." She's not really, no official promotion or title, but Bridget told Keisha that whenever she is here alone on Saturday, Tuesday, and Wednesday nights, she's the manager. And with how business has fallen off on account of White Oaks Mall being the last place people want to spend their evenings, Bridget can't afford more than one girl to be here, is probably losing money at that. She's certainly not too crazy about having to trust Keisha to count down the cash at the end of the night and bundle up the deposit, but Bridget gave her a twenty-five-cent raise to ensure her integrity.

Before Peggy can call bullshit, Keisha says. "We're closed now." The dimes gush from her fingers and crash into

59

the slot, three or four still stuck to the sweat on her open palm. Probably about three dollars. That's what she writes down.

"What are you in such a hurry for? You got some kind of hot plans going on tonight?"

"Nothing," Keisha says. She scoops up the nickels.

"Gina, will you look at this girl and tell me she don't have something special planned after she gets out of here?"

"I like your dress," Gina says. Whether she means it or is making fun of her, Keisha can't be sure. The statement is followed by the chutter of her straw hitting an air pocket.

Keisha thought about wearing a white T-shirt underneath her black floral sundress, at least while she's at work. She saw that look in a catalog once, and some girls do it at school so they don't get called to the office for spaghetti straps, which are technically against the dress code if some teacher wants to call you out on it, never a guy teacher, of course, but sometimes Mrs. Hanscom will, because she is pushing 70 and hasn't had something worth showing off for at least 30 years now, so has to hassle everybody else who does. Keisha feels the freeze of the pumped-in air conditioning on her shoulders. Outside in the mall they are playing, "Crazy in Love." She hears it for the first time just as it's ending. The first nickel clunks into the empty trough.

"Yeah, nobody wears dresses to work at this place," Peggy says. Her hands and those nails are clamped onto the edge of the counter in front of her, maybe to still the shakes. Her eyes behind those lashes are bleeding out. "I've walked by this place and seen them in shorts and T-shirts, like slobs. Now, what are you so dressed up for? Fess up."

Keisha hopes that an answer will get the blonde back to browsing. "This boy is having some of us over. Probably watch a movie. That's all."

60

"Watch a movie?" Peggy exhales upward and snickers. She's onto her. "You ain't dressed up like that to watch no movie. Gina, does she look like she made herself up to watch a goddamn movie?"

"Don't look like it to me," Gina says. "I wouldn't go to that much trouble to watch a movie."

"You didn't go to that much trouble for your wedding. No wonder it didn't last two years."

"Shut up, Peggy."

"I mean, look, she straightened her hair and everything. That must've taken hours. How long it take you?"

"I don't know," Keisha says. "Not long." She retrieves an empty can of Mello Yello that she finished earlier from underneath the counter, and sets it in front of Peggy. "Your ash."

"How do you do it?" Peggy flicks the cigarette into the mouth hole and comes leering over the counter to get a closer look.

"Do what?"

"Do you use an iron or some kind of coconut oil or something else? I always smell coconuts." She reaches over and takes a pinch of Keisha's hair between thumb and forefinger, those acrylic polymer nails scraping and popping down the strands to the end. They always think they got the right. Keisha knocks her orange hand away, but after she's let go anyway. Peggy holds her hand up as if to say okay, okay. She smells her fingers. "See, coconuts. I knew it."

"It's not coconuts."

"Got to be a bitch to straighten out that kink, I'll bet. You probably don't do it every day, do you? Nobody would have that kind of time. I got to know what you do, though. Mine needs something terrible. Look at this. I need help." She

61

scissors her fingers across a tuft of her own hair and razors them downward until only a jagged line of thatch is sticking out. It's the same way a barber holds it before he snips it off. She drops her hair, holds her cigarette tilted toward her mouth, and begins looking over it at the bejeweled eyeglass cases. "Must be a boy on the other end of this night. Got to be for that much trouble." She looks at Keisha for confirmation. "Nobody gets all dressed up and straightens her hair and shows her cha-chas if there ain't no fella might see her."

Keisha tucks her elbows close to her sides, realizes that's only boosting things up, so she rotates away from them as she counts. Peggy can only see her back, Gina a little more if she weren't preoccupied by the Stiletto Press-On Glitter Nails. Keisha considers reminding them of the time again, but she doesn't think it'll stir these two.

"Maybe he doesn't even know you like him, and that's why you're trying so hard. Is that the story?" Keisha sort of shrugs. "He a white boy?" Keisha just drops the next nickel. "Got to be, right?" Peggy says. "In this town. What school do you go to?" Keisha tells her. "Can't be easy just trying to fit in. A girl like you probably has to go all out to compete with the other girls in that school. But you know, if you look hard enough…" She gestures toward Keisha with her cigarette hand. "I'll bet you'd find out some of them boys actually prefer you to them others. Ain't that true?"

Keisha focuses on those nickels, one perched on the side of her finger, Jefferson side up. She reaches with her thumb to push it along into the trough.

"Can we go?" Gina says. She keeps the cup at a safe distance, the rim of her lips and teeth behind them turned to Pepto Bismol pink. "Pick something and let's go. I got to pee,

62

and I want a chicken parmesan." Her knees are smashed together to hold it in.

"No, I haven't found what I'm looking for."

"But I got to go pee. What does it matter anyway if she hates everything? What are you breaking your back for?"

"Jesus, what do you expect if you drink all that? You got a bathroom back there that she could use?" Peggy motions toward the closed door behind the counter.

"No."

"You don't got no bathroom back there? Where do you go?"

"Yeah, we got a bathroom, but no, she can't use it. It isn't for customers."

"Isn't for customers. Give me a break. Just let her go. You're the manager after all. She's not going to pee on the seat or nothing, but she'll sure as shit turn this carpet into a cherry ocean if you don't let her. And drive us both nuts before she does. Once old Gina here realizes she has to go, she won't stop whining about it until she gets to."

Keisha opens the door behind the counter and tells her to go ahead. Gina sets her cup down on the counter and hustles around it and Peggy to the open door behind Keisha, nudges her as she goes by, sending four or five nickels plunking into the drawer. Keisha doesn't give her further directions. The bathroom is off of the dinky office, and she's only got two doors to choose from aside from the gray-painted steel door marked EXIT that leads into the network of hallways running behind the stores and out to the parking lot. Unless she goes into the storage closet by mistake, she should find it just fine.

"Maybe a charm bracelet." Peggy dangles it in front of her face, the smoke floating up through the links. "I could get her a new charm to put on it every time I have to buy her something, every birthday and Christmas too. Then I wouldn't have to go through this every goddamn time I got to buy her a gift. What do you think of that?"

Keisha writes down an estimate on the nickels, and shovels up the pennies, thumbing them into the drawer. "Sure, they're pretty popular." She can't remember ever seeing anyone wearing one, though, except her grandma eight years ago while they played Old Maid in her apartment on the southside of Chicago, which took her mom three hours to drive to. She remembers the massive car wash sign across the street that flashed pink through the patio door into the third-floor apartment day and night, and how those charms of the Eiffel Tower, the Statue of Liberty, and Mount Rushmore made Keisha wonder if she had been to all those places. They tinkled together whenever her grandmother reached to take from Keisha's hand one of the cards which were so ancient and muddy you could barely tell if you had a match or even the death card. That one and only visit ended shortly after the second game when despite her grandma's insistence they stay, Keisha's mom said they really needed to leave, but by any chance, did she have an extra five hundred dollars she could spare because the fridge conked out on them two days ago with no money to fix it. As her grandma counted out the mopey bills from a cigar box she kept behind her bread box, Keisha thought of the cereal she'd eaten that morning and how the milk had seemed plenty cold to her.

"How's your daddy feel about it, about you and this boy?" She's stopped even looking for something for the girl's birthday.

Keisha once again loses count, drops the rest into the slot and writes down 45, close enough. She wishes she'd denied there being a boy. Mitchell Ramona is really nobody more than

64

someone she likes okay who's nice to her in World Studies class and is going to be around tonight, nobody she would ever bring home.

"Can't be too crazy about it, right?" She reaches across and nudges Keisha's elbow. "But he's got to know where he lives—Hell, just walk this mall and he's got to know that—so he's got to expect that when his little girl brings home a boy, that that boy's going to be a certain way, whether he likes it or not." She waits on Keisha's confirmation, but the silence confirms something else. "Oh, I bet I know what's going on here." She is nodding her head, oh yes. "You can't say how your daddy feels because there's no daddy to speak of." Peggy gets it. As her deduction brings a smile, Keisha turns to see it, the enamel turned gray and furrowed like tree bark scorched by the winter. People who come across Peggy for the first time probably think she's half pretty, roots or no roots, until she smiles. That smile is something else, like standing at the edge of a dying forest, and all you want to do is run the other way.

Keisha thinks of denying it. Sure, she has one. Then she thinks of blaming his absence on brain cancer or a drunk driver he never saw coming while she and her mom waited for him at home with a pot roast cooking in the oven. Lay it on her like that, and fuck her for assuming it was just a typical case of a sixteen-year-old girl being charmed out of her panties at the drive-in and left holding the bag, the father cutting out because that's all they know how to do. Now, sixteen years later, the two look more like sisters than mother and daughter, and only a matter of time before the daughter gets herself into the same kind of trouble because that's how she's been taught life is supposed to go.

Keisha doesn't say anything, though, doesn't have it in her. Her mom went out tonight with some guy she met at the

Blockbuster two days ago as they both reached for the same copy of *Remember the Titans*, and if that wasn't fate, she didn't know what was.

Gina neglected to shut the door all the way, and they can both hear her urine drilling a hole through the porcelain. She's moaning.

He's an exterminator, the guy her mother met at Blockbuster, and he's taking her to dinner at The Ground Round, the place in the strip mall on Route 4 where they give you a bowl of free peanuts while you wait for your food, and let you throw the empty shells right on the floor so that they crunch under your feet when you walk to the bathroom. It has the makings of an early evening, except knowing her mom, Keisha will be returning to an empty house, no matter how many movies they watch at Calvin Skoakley's house. When everyone calls it a night because they're expected home, Keisha will have to pretend she has a curfew too.

II

Keisha backs away from the register and lets the drawer slide open all the way. She can't wait anymore. She grabs the twenties and begins running them from hand to hand.

Peggy notices. "You guys made a haul today. I didn't think anybody came in here buying this crap, but you must've been busy all day."

"Saturdays and Christmas shopping," Keisha says.

"You ever think of skimming a little for yourself?"

"What?"

"All that, they'd never miss it."

"I don't do that."

"Got to pay you shit here, right? You got it coming to you. Nobody would blame you."

"No...they got cameras out here, and even if they didn't, I wouldn't do it."

She takes a drag as if it doesn't matter one way or another, but holds onto the register slots. "They don't got cameras everywhere, do they? Only one out here as far as I can see." She's referring to a lens embedded conspicuously in the ceiling above the counter, which Keisha is pretty sure is nothing but a prop to deter skimming and shoplifting with no actual camera behind it. Even if there is some camera up there, Keisha doubts Bridget finds the time to watch six hours of footage each day to make sure her employees are honest after she leaves in the evening.

"There's not one in that office, I'll bet," Peggy says. "Got to be blind spots all over the place. Just saying, they'd never know if you ever did take what you're due."

67

"I wouldn't do that. My boss would know. She expects the drawer to be to the penny."

"Well, she doesn't need to know. There are other ways." Peggy seems to forget the suggestion and rediscovers the previous topic. "Got to be rough on you, g—" She catches herself, sucks on her cigarette. "No daddy to tell you how it is. I know. Mine got sick of being married to my mom just about the time I was going into second grade, but at least I still got to sleep over at his apartment every couple weeks on a couch that smelled of cat piss. Lucky me." She looks hard across the store at something on the other end and stays on it. Keisha has seen her mom freeze up like this while sitting in front of the TV in the evenings, after the ice in her third or fourth vodka has gone to cotton on the surface, and one of the J's that she bought from the delivery boy at the pet store where she works has burnt itself out to a stub in her forked fingers. She will be locked onto the screen, unblinking, the pictures playing in her eyes, with Keisha sitting next to her afraid to ask if anything is wrong.

Peggy eventually shrugs it off and continues. "Then he met this skag who didn't like kids, at least somebody else's kids, and that ended that. Didn't see him again until he showed up fifteen years later to give me away, the fat old fuck. A father's duty and all." She shakes her head. "Turns out he was giving me away to the only man on this earth worse than him. I give Gina shit about her go of it, but my little boy's daddy didn't even make it a year. Vamoose." She heaves in a drag, holds it like it's weed, and then lets it unroll over her top lip. "If only he had stuck…"

Her statement gives way to silence. Her focus drifts toward the storefront and the railing she almost fell over while wondering the name of that toy store. She is probably still

68

trying to come up with it. Keisha can't bring herself to move the next bill. She holds them until Peggy shakes it off. "Okay, how about him then? How about his dad, that boy's dad? How does his dad feel about you and...what's his name?"

"Mitchell."

"That his first or last name?"

"First."

"*Mitchell*...A name like Mitchell, he's got to have two parents and a perfect life. How does Mitchell's dad feel about you coming in their door? I hate to say it, but it's probably a tough nut for him. He's probably thinking in a whole city of girls, his boy brings home—"

"Brings home what?"

"Nothing, you know what I mean."

"Never met him, so I can't say."

"Well, be ready. That's how they think, dads. I ain't saying it's right or anything, but you got to be ready for that kind of reaction."

"What about you?" She reaches the bottom twenty, but isn't sure if she counted seven or eight, so she has to start again.

"Me?"

"Yeah, you. How would you feel if your boy...Tommy, right?" Peggy drops her chin in confirmation. "How would you feel if Tommy brought me home?" Keisha locks on her. She imagines her and Tommy entering this chick's doublewide with their arms crossed around each other and her fingers tucked into his back pocket so he can't pull away to lessen the impact.

"Well, I wouldn't have to worry about that—"

"Worry about it." Keisha exhales hard through her nose.

"That's not what I mean. I mean it couldn't happen..." She sucks on her cigarette instead of finishing, those sun cracks deepening along her upper lip. She picks up a can of glitter mousse and proceeds to read the label closely.

"Because he wouldn't go out with me?" She almost slaps the word at the end as an exclamation, like the rhinestone on Peggy's middle finger and not just fuck you, but double fuck you. Saying it to her would only give her something, though, verify something she's been wondering since wandering in here.

"No—"

"He wouldn't go out with one, huh?"

"No, that's not it. That's not what I'm saying. He would. Of course, he would. I got nothing against you. You seem sweet enough. And you're pretty. Real pretty. Of course, he would." She goes to set the can down, but it tumbles off the shelf onto the floor. She bends down to retrieve it, watches her hands put it back into the space as if it's a crystal champagne flute she is returning to a shelf stacked with them, and if she doesn't place it just right... "I'm sure he would. I'm sure he'd have no problem with it. No problem at all." The cigarette twitters between her fingers. The paper is gashed on one side and threatens to tear down the center and spill out the last inch of tobacco.

"Is that so?" Out there in the mall, the LEDs recessed far above in the ceiling have dimmed a couple shades, like the color of enamel that surrounds a twenty-year-old steel filling. The Muzak drifting from the ceiling cuts out. Keisha couldn't have named the song that was interrupted, didn't even register it was playing at all except in the sudden empty tunnel left behind.

"Well," Peggy says. "I guess I can't be sure." She takes refuge in her cigarette, tries her best to suck the cherry through the filter.

70

Keisha sees the descent of her features and wants to shift the conversation away from where it is, back to the charm bracelet that Peggy has already moved on from. The two of them are talking about different things, but Keisha can't help herself. "Didn't think so."

Peggy's speech is untriggered, "I said, I don't know."

Gina emerges from the back, and Keisha can't recall hearing a flush. "Thanks. God, I was dying." She turns to Peggy, who's entranced by the shelf of mousse, the nearly cashed out cigarette sagging from her lips. "Did you find something?...What's wrong?" When she doesn't get a reply from Peggy, she turns the question toward Keisha.

"It's your friend, ask her."

Gina rounds the corner and asks her what's going on, places a hand on her bare back, that tangerine blouse riding extra low to show a crumpled pouch of cleavage. "Pick something and let's go. The mood ring. She'll like that."

"Tommy," Peggy says.

"Tommy? Your Tommy?"

"Of course, my Tommy."

"Oh, how did you get to talking about that? We're here for Trisha, remember?" She turns to Keisha. "What you got to go and bring up Tommy for? Now she's all down and out about it. Look at her. It's my only night out in two weeks, and now you got her all sad."

"I just asked her about Tommy. How am I supposed to know you're not supposed to bring up Tommy? She brought him up first. I don't even know Tommy." She juggles the name like something hot she can't touch too long, but can't let drop either. She writes down a jittery 120 for the tens.

Peggy's tracing something on the countertop with her nail.

71

Gina picks up her drink from the counter, takes a swig and then holds it out from her curling-up mouth as if discovering someone spiked it. "Just get something for Trisha, and let's get out of here."

"Ungrateful brat. I'm stuck buying for her when…" She is rolling her head back and forth, and her eyes squinch at the corners. She flicks the ash off into the hole of the Mello Yellow can, papery flecks dropping onto the counter and sticking to the residual moisture from Keisha's wipe down.

"Well, buy her anything, and let's go get Rum Runners. It's my only night out. Let's not get all down about it."

"Rum Runners at Ruby Tuesdays?" She looks up at Keisha as if for some confirmation. "You hear this, Keisha? If, when you ever grow up, you realize that your biggest thrill in life has become Rum Runners at the Ruby Tuesdays, climb to the top of the highest building you can find, and throw yourself off." She deposits her cashed-out cigarette into the hole atop the can. "Promise me, you'll do that. Okay, Keisha?" She descends onto the corner of one of the white pedestals and sits next to a turnstile. She retrieves the mangled cigarette pack from her purse, fingers inside for another, but comes up empty.

"Oh, Christ," Gina says. "We'll take this." She pulls a mood ring from the rack and holds it up for Peggy. "You like these, right? She'll like this."

Peggy doesn't even look up. Her arms are propped in a diamond across her thighs so that her hands meet between her knees, her fingers forked where there should've been a cigarette if she hadn't run out. "She'll hate it."

"Not more than anything else."

Gina holds out a hand to Peggy, who dumbly produces a rolled $20 that might be the last bill she has on this earth.

Keisha unrolls it. It's wet. She flattens the bill out into the slot and gives Gina the change for 15.49. She can make change in her head and add to the pile, but now her counts are all off.

"Can you get rid of this?" Gina says, a groan in her voice as she relinquishes the remainder of her cup with four inches of pink foam at the bottom. "It's going to make me sick."

She sets it on the edge of the counter, but doesn't quite make it, and the cup tumbles off the edge on her side, making a boom as it hits the floor and cannonballs the lid off. Keisha can't see the impact point from where she's standing, but she sees the shrapnel spotting the nearby surfaces, and the perimeter of the red puddle oozing over the floor into her view.

"Oh Je-sus," Gina says, stretching out the name as if she's really seeing a vision of the savior right there in Claire's and doesn't know what to do about it. The pill must be hitting her. She steps back.

"Are you serious?" Peggy says. She comes back to reality. "You got it on my jeans." She tilts her ankle up to show her. "Will you look at that? Look at that. All over my jeans." Keisha can't see anything amid the bleach spots. Those white strappy sandals are the only part that Keisha likes about her outfit, except they don't cover the blue worms bulging up along the top of her feet. Peggy must've been on her feet working a counter for a lot of years, and now the blood collects in her shoes.

"It'll come out. Sorry, it was an accident."

"I bet you're sorry." Wetness collects in her bottom lids, rainwater overflowing from a garage gutter because

73

somewhere down below, the downspout is clogged with leaves and dirt.

Keisha can't imagine ever crying for those jeans.

"It was an accident." She retrieves the cup, reapplies the lid and hands it over to Keisha to deposit in the trash. "You saw it. It was an accident."

Keisha closes the drawer with the fives and ones still uncounted, and goes around the counter to see the red foamy swamp between the counter and the hoop earring turnstile, sizzling as it sinks into the gray rug.

"Ah, hell no." She retrieves a rag from behind the counter and comes back around. "It says no drinking in here." Too late to lay down the law now.

"Sorry," Gina says, like a girl whose mom orders her to apologize for something she doesn't really think she did or doesn't think is all that bad and why should she have to?

"Looks like somebody came in here," Peggy says. "And blew their ever-fucking brains out." Keisha comes over with the rag. "Oh no, you don't," Peggy says. "Keisha, why should you have to clean this up? She'll take care of it. Not you. Why should you? She's the one who spilled it. Oaf." She pulls the rag from Keisha and slaps it into Gina's hand.

"Fine," Gina says. "I'll do it, but don't call me no oaf." She lowers herself to her knees, tugging at the back hem of her skirt so her can doesn't spring free. She presses the rag into the center to soak it up. More of her chubby thighs are showing than she probably planned on with that outfit. As she works, she tugs down on her skirt every few seconds.

"Just go on with what you got to do to close. Gina spends most of each day on her knees anyway. It's what she does for a living."

74

"Scrubbing tubs. That's what she means. At the Royal Motor Lodge...the one on Route 4. I do housekeeping, not nothing else."

"Sure, scrubbing tubs. That's why you haul in those tips, and why you can't stop sucking on that straw. Mother Theresa scrubbing tubs. Well, put your skills to good use."

In thirty seconds, the rag turns into a bloody cut of beef. It doesn't do anything except push the color in. She hands the sodden thing back to Keisha, the strawberry running down both their arms. She holds the rag far from her dress and throws it out with the cup.

"Get another rag there, Keisha, maybe two. It's already looking better. She'll get it all up for you. You won't even know where she spilled it when she's done."

Gina tucks a thatch of stringy hair behind her ear, and observes the splotch in front of her. She begins dabbing at the rug. "I don't know, Peggy."

Peggy takes the two clean rags from Keisha and drops them onto the stain. "Of course you do. You can't imagine what Gina here has to mop up from the carpet at the Motor Lodge. Some nasty-ass shit going on there. This ain't nothing for her. Now hurry up. Keisha here has got hot plans with old Mitchell tonight, and we are holding her up." She flicks a hand Keisha's way. "You go on and finish up your counting, and go ahead and take a little for yourself. You've earned it, having to deal with the likes of us two."

"I don't do that."

"What else you got to do to close up?"

"Run the sweeper over the floor."

"I'll tell you what. I'll push the sweeper out here, and you get to work on that drawer."

It's going on 9:20. Keisha gives Peggy the sweeper, who takes the handle from her as if she's just been handed a loaded gun for the first time, and isn't sure which end the bullet comes out of.

"Where do you turn it on?"

"You don't," Gina says from below them. "Just roll it over the carpeting." She glances back at Keisha. "Just imagine what her apartment looks like."

"Shut up and scrub, Gina."

"Can't scrub it," she says. "Breaks down the fibers if you do that." Her voice sounds floaty.

"Fuck do we care, broken fibers. Jesus." Peggy moves the sweeper up and down a section of carpet to test it out. "That's it?" she says.

"That's it." She is going to do a shit job, no doubt, and Keisha should just tell them to leave, and maybe they would now, since they have the gift for her girl and all, but there's something about putting them both to work and her being able to watch, while counting money like the boss. She can't resist it.

"I guess it works," she says.

Keisha punches the drawer open. All she's got are ones and fives left, but she can't be sure about any of her counts, so when she takes the drawer to the back, she'll need to start over. Bridget wants it to the penny.

"How many people are coming to this party?" Peggy has run the sweeper across the same strip of carpet between the rack of headbands and bin of endangered stuffed animals about two dozen times now, doesn't seem to understand you have to move around the store.

"It isn't a party. It's just a few people coming over to watch a movie."

76

"It's a party," Peggy says. "That's a party dress."

"It's not a party."

"Well, we could make it a party." She props herself on the sweeper. "I'll tell you what. Let's go and pick up some cocktails from the packaged place and deliver it. I'll guarantee none of your friends will even turn on a movie after that. Get them all up dancing and going all wild. You wore a party dress. Let's make it a party."

Keisha stalls on $35 in fives, answers after a pause. "It's not that kind of crowd." She can imagine showing up with a couple cases of something delivered by these two middle-aged skanks with nothing better to do on a Friday night than contribute to the delinquency of minors.

"Not that kind of crowd. Bunch of stiffs, huh. Getting all dressed up and straightening your hair to hang out with a tight-ass bunch of white kids."

"This ain't coming out," Gina says.

"Keep at it, and give me a Kool." The sweeper is not moving. She takes a cigarette from her friend and lights it, basks in the glorious first inhale. Then the lousy bitch ashes right on the rug and sweeps it up. "Well, if you don't have no party to go to. How's about we make one here?" She reaches into her purse and comes out with two nips clasped between her forked fingers.

Gina looks up from her place on the floor. "Where'd you get those?"

"Where do you think? Got any glasses?"

Keisha lags in answering, but then returns with three coffee mugs Bridget keeps around for the employees to make coffee or tea during break.

"Oh yes, perfect." Peggy leans the handle of the sweeper next to a pedestal and comes over to the counter. "I

77

work at Wolfie's Liquor, and every night, I help myself to a little sampling on my way out. You got to take the perks where you can get 'em." She cracks open the two bottles of Old Forester and dumps one in each mug, leaving the third empty. She slides one over to Keisha. "It's not the good stuff, but hey."

Gina reaches up from below, but receives nothing. "Hey, where's mine?"

"You couldn't even handle that cherry soda."

"It's strawberry, and yes, I could."

"Get back to work, so we can get Keisha out of here." She clinks her mug against Keisha's, and the two take simultaneous drinks. Keisha's is just a sip that unzips her throat. She deposits the empties into the can below the counter, makes a mental note to haul it to the dumpster on her way out so that Bridget doesn't stumble on them in the morning.

Peggy returns to her sweeper. "Ah, this does make closing so much better." She begins to lunge forward and back with the sweeper, knocking a Formica pedestal and rattling the contents above it. Gina works on the stain, and Keisha goes back to counting, flushing down a sip every so often. They go on like this for the next few minutes, Keisha counting the bills and recounting the change so the deposit is to the penny for Bridget, Peggy finally making her way around the store. She's humming something, but each time the notes start to string together into something Keisha can almost recognize, Peggy cuts out to take a drink from her mug, leaving Keisha to wait for Peggy to start again.

III

Keisha is writing the last of her figures and adding them up with the calculator that sits next to the register when she just asks, "What happened to Tommy?" She's pretty sure he's not around anymore to buy birthday presents for, or anything else. It's so strange when a person is there for so long and then isn't anymore. Like what happened two years ago to Ryan Kershing, who was twelve years old riding home from the skate park and never made it. They're sure somebody grabbed him. They never even found his board. Since the second grade, Keisha rode the bus with him. Then one day she didn't. It doesn't seem possible, him disappearing like that, and it makes you want to know why and how. How could that happen to a person? Based on Peggy's reaction to those kids out there, Keisha thinks whatever happened to her Tommy was similar to what happened to Ryan Kershing. Here to find out, she's both sort of right and not right at all.

"Tommy…" The sweeper stops, and Peggy dumps the already empty mug into her mouth. She produces another bottle and drains it into her mug without offering Keisha some. This empty she sets on the nearest surface, another thing Keisha will have to remember to retrieve later.

"Tommy," Gina says. She is on her knees, a strawberry rag held out from her body. "Don't bring him up. This isn't coming out. Let's go. I'll pay for it to be cleaned. Let me know how much, and I'll send you a cheque for it." Sure, she will.

"He's at Pontiac."

"Pontiac?"

"Pontiac…lockup…Pontiac Correctional."

"Oh Pegs," Gina says.

"He's never getting out."

Keisha hits the wrong key on the calculator and has to clear it to start over. Her finger doesn't hit the next button. She just stands there. Somewhere outside the gate, she can hear the tornado of the floor scrubber that the custodians ride around like a Zamboni after close.

Her lips are puckered as she goes on, so that her words take on a kazoo quality. "He broke a kid's neck, all right? A seven-year-old. Then threw him into the Davies River. Now I got to piss." She drops the handle of the sweeper and without asking, rushes past Keisha into the back, the hollow door inside the office slamming home.

"That's not all." Gina is up on her knees, a pulpy rag in her hand. She is hushed as she goes on. "The day that that Winston boy went missing, Tommy never showed up to work in the morning. He snatched the poor kid right from his front yard and took him out to this Boy Scout Camp that was closed up for the winter, kept him there in some cabin for about seven or eight hours before he killed him." She pauses to let that sink in. "Now they got to put him in a separate wing at Pontiac so that nobody can get ahold of him because they'll kill him otherwise. They don't like his kind." Gina looks toward the closed door to the back. "You know the saddest part about it, Peggy had to know something like that was coming. 'Cause her next boyfriend after Tommy's father split, this lowlife Neil, he was doing the same thing to Tommy for months before Peggy found out and kicked him to the curb. Somebody does something like that to a kid, you got to expect that kid to be off. You got to expect he ain't going to grow up to be alright.

"One afternoon when he was about ten—that was when Neal was still living with them and still at it—Peggy sent

Tommy out to her garden because the green caterpillars were all over her tomato plants and eating them to shreds. She told him she'd give him a quarter for each one he caught, and gave him a cleaned-out mayonnaise jar to put them in. Well, the kid comes back with about thirty of them crawling around in that jar, and after his mom gives him the money, he starts shaking the jar up and down like he's mixing a martini, and those things start bursting against the sides. He has this shit-eating grin on his face while he's doing it. He's having a great time. By the time he was done, the whole inside of the jar was covered in yellow and green caterpillar guts. It was disgusting. It was horrible." The toilet flushes inside, and Gina hastens her story. "I saw that jar, and I knew the kid wasn't right. For as long as I knew him, he never was. Talk to the kid for five minutes, you knew that. I just didn't know why. When Peggy finally discovered what Neil was doing, I understood why. Somebody does something like that to your boy, you can't never repair him. What Tommy ended up doing to that Winston boy. That was only a matter of time."

Peggy reemerges. "I was wrong. She did piss on the seat. You did piss on the seat. I sat right in it. Thanks, a whole helluva a lot. I got my ass all wet."

"Sorry," Gina says.

Keisha says, "We're closed now. Thanks for helping me and all, but I got to close the gate and get out of here." Now she knew what happened to Ryan Kershing, same thing that happened to that Winston boy, or at least something close.

"I'm not done yet," Peggy says, although she sounds entirely disinterested in continuing. "And Gina sure ain't got that stain up yet."

"I don't know, Peggy. I don't think it's ever coming up."

81

"Just keep at it."

"I can finish," Keisha says.

"No way. We're not going to leave you with all this."

Keisha finally manages a total that she's relatively sure about: $646.21. The total that the machine printed on the register tape says $535.54. She calculates the difference: 110.67. She watches the two of them, Gina on her hands and knees scrubbing now, though she warned against that method, and Peggy running the sweeper between drinks and drags. When Peggy eventually returns her gape, Keisha jerks her focus downward toward the slip of paper again, and the pen in her hand hovering over it.

She pulls out the cash drawer, taking it and her calculations back into the office. She shouldn't leave the two of them out in the store unattended, but they're busy enough that she's reasonably sure they won't start stuffing their pockets, not any more than the middle school sneaks who think nobody is onto them making repeated deposits into their purses. Sometimes Keisha maneuvers between a girl and the door to demand she empty the loot from her purse, and threatens to call the cops, but other times, Keisha just lets the dirty little thief scoot right out the front into the mall as if none the wiser. Just depends on her mood, how much the girl tries to take, and whether or not she thinks the girl will scare easily.

Of the occasional black girls who wander into Claire's, Keisha only ever caught one trying to make off with merchandise. The girl looked about twelve, and had pocketed a pair of earrings that cost three bucks. Keisha hates to admit it, but she grabbed the girl's arm like she had never laid her hands on any of the other thieving girls, and worked her over good by telling her how the cops were already on their way, how as soon as they arrived, they were going to arrest her and take her directly to jail where they'd make her spend the night. Keisha should've wanted the girl to be so scared she'd never try it again in some other store run by some white bastard who might lock her in a room and bust her lip open or knock out a tooth, or do about anything else he wanted to her before calling the cops, and prosecuting her to the fullest extent of the law. Keisha would've liked that to be why she laid it on the girl like that, but the real reason was because she couldn't begin to rattle those white girls with a threat of the cops like she could this one, who'd undoubtedly been warned about them as soon as she was old enough to understand her place in the world. She probably feared them more than the boogeyman who lived in the shadows of her basement, or the stranger who would try to talk her into the back of his white van like he had Ryan Kershing, with promises of puppies and strawberry ice cream.

Her reaction had exceeded Keisha's expectations. She started wailing right there in the middle of the store, and saying she was sorry, so, so sorry, that she'd never done it before, that she'd never do it again, she promised, to please not call the police, that she'd pay for it, she'd pay for it right now, just please don't call them. Even after Keisha let go of her because the whole store was gawking at the scene, and told her just to go on home and never do it again, the girl persisted in sobbing and apologizing and holding out three dollars as if Keisha even wanted it anymore. All Keisha wanted from the girl right then was for her to leave already.

Keisha closes the office door behind her. She probably should leave it open to let them know she could pop back out anytime now, but she doesn't want one of them eyeing her through the crack, or seeing the location of the wall safe behind the rolling filing cabinet. She sits down at the desk containing two framed pictures. One is of Bridget's husband Hank hoisting up their daughter Heather to grab an apple from a cluster of them sagging from the high branch of a tree. A bushel basket sits on the ground at his feet. The other is of Bridget and her daughter and son riding their bikes. The boy, whose name is Steven, is laughing at his mom trying to be a daredevil by kicking her legs out in front of her. Heather is gripping for dear life onto the handlebars of her Strawberry Shortcake bike, too busy fearing sudden death to appreciate her mom finally letting loose and acting all crazy.

Bridget isn't even looking at the camera in that one, can't make eye contact, but Keisha turns both pictures face down onto the desk. She looks back at the still-closed door before taking out the list of figures and then the stack of bills. She removes three twenties, two tens, four fives, and ten singles, rubber bands them, and then collects two quarters, a dime, a nickel, and two pennies. She scans the perimeter of the office that extends no more than ten feet in any direction, and tucks the rubber-banded stack and coins, along with her calculations, into the inner side pocket of her purse and zips it. The take has gone up nearly every time, and she is aware that she needs to pull it back, that there is a tipping point at which the money will be missed, when Stephanie's totals on her nights will be too different from Keisha's. She's not sure where that tipping point is, but she thinks it must be close, or maybe has already passed. Each time a customer brings something to the counter though, it's becoming harder and harder to ring it in. Each time she does, that's money not going to her.

She writes down the total, $535.67, onto the top deposit slip, peels it from the stack and sticks everything else from the drawer into a deposit bag, zipping it up. After glancing again at the door, she pushes the filing cabinet aside to reveal the iron safe embedded in the wall. She pulls out the deposit hatch and drops the bag down into the deposit slot of a safe that is just big enough to hold it. Then she returns the filing cabinet to its proper place. She writes down the deposit total into the ledger and leaves the empty drawer on the desk to be filled with change tomorrow.

She stands up with the purse on her shoulder and turns toward the door, nothing more to do than empty the trash and get these two out of here. A corner shelf is stacked haphazardly with binders spilling papers containing yellowed, defunct sales charts and new employee information. She stalls to observe it. One of the binders is leaning against the next with a triangular gap in between, and as she pivots toward the door, that shadowy triangle winks at her. She reverses direction, and it happens again.

She approaches the two binders and spreads them apart, knocking the one on the end to the floor with a spasm of papers. There, sitting on the shelf in the space, is a video camera as big as a shoe box. The thing had been tucked away in the shadows, the red light previously obscured by one of the binders stacked around it. It's trained on the desk. So that's what Bridget thinks of her.

Keisha picks up the thing. It's just a VHS camera—they probably haven't been sold anywhere for a decade, and all she can remember from recording movies on her VCR at home is that it can record for six hours if you set it for SLP and don't mind the picture being a little jumpy. Bridget must've set this up before she dragged herself out of here this afternoon, probably has been doing that since business started to slump, and she had no choice but to leave Keisha or Stephanie here to close by herself. What Keisha wants to know is if Bridget goes to this much trouble when it's Stephanie here doing the closing.

Peggy barks something at Gina out in the store, and Gina issues some protest, which prompts Peggy to crack open with laughter, the laugh of a woman whose son did what hers did, all on account of her getting a little too lonely way back when and inviting any filthy bastard into their home to fill up the space. Now her son is gone forever, the filthy bastard has been replaced, and she's here shopping at the mall for somebody else's kid she can't even stand. All you can do with that is laugh.

Keisha hits stop on the camera and then ejects the tape from the side. There are no wires feeding the footage somewhere else. She rotates the TDK tape. This is the evidence. This is it. In the corner is a TV/VCR combo on which Keisha watched at least three hours of customer service and product videos when she was first hired.

Each morning before raising the gate, Bridget must pop in the tape from the night before and over her coffee, observe Keisha on that television, counting money to make sure every bill and every coin goes from the drawer into that bag and that bag into the wall. If it doesn't, she'll know. The only reason Keisha is still working here is because she takes care of her business out there behind the counter before heading back into the office. She would've done it the same way tonight had there not been those two skanks lagging out there.

She knows just how to hunch forward in front of the register and slide the excess money for all the purchases she never rang up that evening down the front of her rib cage and into the purse tucked there, so that if the lens embedded in the ceiling does actually have a working camera attached to it, if it really is recording her throughout her shift, the pivotal moments will show nothing more than footage of her back.

She's never done anything in this office they can get you on, not until tonight. Something about being in this office. There is that gray door leading to the back hallways through which Bridget might pop in at any moment, has done just that on some occasions because she happened to be in the neighborhood and figured she'd stop by to see how things are going, and does Keisha need any help with anything? Of course, she was in the neighborhood. She lives in this neighborhood.

Keisha always thought it was the pictures that bothered her, but maybe she's been feeling that glass eye on her all along. She has to expect that. Whether she's digging through the bargain bin of two-dollar cassettes at JR's Music, sorting through the discounted clothes at TJ Maxx, or just walking to The White Hen two blocks from her house, there's always somebody watching her.

Keisha takes a moment to consider what now. She can take the tape with her, but then Bridget will wonder why it's gone. A better thing to do is just record over the incriminating portion, and then return the camera to the hidden place on the shelf as if Keisha were still in the dark. Bridget might make something of the skip in the footage or the invariable shift in the focus, but if it bothers her too much, the most she can do with that is fire Keisha for some trumped-up bullshit, maybe that red splotch in the carpet and why does she think they have a sign that says no food or drink inside? Bridget would probably still give a decent reference to the next place she applied to.

Keisha is still holding the camera in one hand and the tape in the other like a balance scale, as the gray-painted exit door swings open, and coming in from the employee hallways is Bridget. There she is. Her blonde hair is gnarled up in a head kerchief which only serves to accentuate her eyes, still skid-marked with last night's waterproof eyeliner, her cheeks sucked downward as if she were making an ascent to the top floor of a skyscraper in a supersonic elevator. She is not in good health. She's wearing a moth-eaten Northwestern sweatshirt from the school her younger sister attended about a decade ago, but never got through her first year because, as Bridget tells it, her sister was more interested in bongs than biology, and last Keisha heard, is a Bank One drive-thru teller.

The two stand there at either side of the office with a wheelie chair and four feet of rug between them. Each examines the other without moving, a couple of girls standing off in the middle of the cafeteria who, after exhausting themselves hollering threats and insults, are wondering who between them will throw the first blow. Bridget says her name across the space as if surprised to run into Keisha here. She lets the door fall closed behind her.

"You were recording me," Keisha says.

Bridget's throat bucks, and she looks like she might dry heave, probably has been doing so all day. "I didn't..." She has to swallow to keep it down. "I wasn't..." She can't finish.

"Isn't that against the law, to stick a camera behind some books and record someone without them knowing?"

"No...no, I don't believe so. I was just—" Bridget grasps onto the doorknob because her knee sort of gives out. This is more than a few too many Cosmos last night. To think this store can survive on the weekly allowance of middle-school girls. Claire's isn't going to make it. It's going under like the rest of the stores in this mall, even if every penny does go into the safe at the end of the night. It'll never be enough. Bridget knows exactly what's coming.

"You don't trust me." Keisha wants to lay that on her, let it swell in her squishy brain, at least for another minute or two.

"Of course, I do."

"No, you don't. You don't trust me. You never did. You probably felt like you needed to hire me, but you never wanted to."

"Of course, I wanted to. I wouldn't have hired you if I didn't want to. You've worked out great here. We need you."

"Funny way of showing it."

No matter how offended she can act, there is still the business of the tape. A solution to everything comes to Keisha. She sets the camera down on the desk and takes the tape in her fists, tries to wrench the fucker in half. When that doesn't work, she lifts a knee and tries to crack it in two. Outrage made her do it. It's perfectly understandable if some suspicious bitch thinks no better of you. When you find out she's recording you, you got to do something to let her know you don't approve.

The tape is one motherfucking indestructible piece of plastic, though. It stays in one piece. It's unbreakable. There are other things she could've done that she'll think of later, like stomping on it or ripping the ribbon of tape free from the roll.

Bridget says something, probably her name again, but Keisha only hears the tick-tick-tick of some cart being rolled through hallways with a lazy wheel, likely the final load of trash from the Orange Julius three stores down, heading to the dumpsters out back.

The sound fades away, and Keisha latches onto her purse as if Bridget might snatch it from her arm and start rooting around inside. Maybe she can see the square shape bulging through the side, confirming that her suspicions have been right all along. She skimmed almost a quarter of what they made today. It's so obvious. It's too much.

Her mother has never asked Keisha to contribute, except when she occasionally comes up short on the cable bill for which she will usually pay her daughter back the next Friday. Her mom calls out of work every couple of weeks when she just doesn't feel up to going in that day, but the owner of Paws Inc. must have a soft spot for her because he hasn't fired her yet. Maybe he's scared of a discrimination suit if he does. Keisha saved for a year to buy that Datsun she drives, and she paid for the thing outright. She can't think of anything else she's saving up for. Her hand falls to the side of her purse. Tomorrow, it would've been more. It would never be enough.

Tape still in hand, Keisha makes the great escape. She swivels from Bridget and bursts from the office into the store. She rounds the counter, and both Peggy and Gina behold her entrance. *"Run,"* she tells them for no particular reason. They have no reason to, except maybe the damage to the carpet, which was just an accident anyway.

She repeats the order. Inexplicably, they do what she says, Peggy welcoming a reason to drop the sweeper handle, and Gina vaulting up from the floor and the stain that is never coming out no matter how much experience she has on her knees. They chase after Keisha as she weaves through the narrow space between the racks, her elbow toppling a turnstile of dangling earrings glitteringly onto the floor. She doesn't stop, but ducks beneath the gate into the grim empty space of the mall. The Zamboni is grinding up the tile floor somewhere on the second level. She can't see it from here. She's fired, or she quit, either one, but that's it. As long as she has this tape, that's all Bridget can do to her.

She flees past the Fig tree that is growing too big for its planter and looks like it might tip over.

"Where?" Peggy says.

Keisha answers the question Peggy should've been asking. "My boss…the owner."

"The owner," Peggy says. Her black lungs are already puffing, but she and Gina are locked in on where this is going. Maybe a chase is just what their evening needed. They'll see this one to the end.

Keisha makes for the escalator. Somewhere behind her, Bridget has emerged from the office and is calling after her, calling her to wait, that she's sorry, to come back, please, Keisha, come back. She needs her. She doesn't sound like Keisha would have expected her to in this situation, not like a boss who caught you on the take and is bringing the cops in on this, will take every necessary punitive step to make sure you learn your lesson and never rip off somebody again. Didn't you see she was just trying to give you a break by hiring you, when most of these store owners would've dumped your application as soon as they read your name written on the top line?

Bridget sounds more like the black girl who had to beg Keisha for her life over a three-dollar pair of earrings. This is the way the mother of that boy, Winston, whose name Keisha somehow remembers, how she must've sounded as she called to him across the neighborhood when she realized he wasn't kicking a ball across the front yard anymore. He had been right there just a minute ago, she must've assured herself, so he couldn't be too far. Or how Peggy must've sounded when she called to Tommy one last time from the back of the courtroom as the verdict came down, knowing her son's verdict had been her verdict all along, and for the rest of her life, she'd never again see the light of day.

The escalator is off, but Keisha starts down the still steel-combed steps. Peggy and Gina are right behind her, making their way to the main level. Bridget is above them, issuing the same pleas, but already losing steam.

Keisha hits the bottom and glances up to see Bridget standing against the railing beside the escalator. She isn't coming down.

Keisha cuts right toward the closest exit, but stalls near the coin fountain. Turned off, it is nothing more than a pool of water with coins coating the bottom, most of them pennies probably begged away from the bottom of Mom's purse or Dad's front pocket in the hopes of a wish being granted if you thought hard enough as the coin plopped through the surface and seesawed down to the bottom. The pennies gleam from soaking so long in the chlorinated pool that the copper looks pink.

Keisha's Datsun is parked near the upstairs entrance, and she will have to go up the stairwell outside Sears and then out the upper entrance. Then she'll have to walk around the outside of the building to get to it. She just isn't sure where to go from there. To Calvin's house, she guesses. That's what she planned, but she suddenly can't imagine sitting silently through a movie among those other kids, none of whom will notice her dress among everyone else's jeans, probably not even Mitchell, or have any idea how much she went through to get her hair to hang straight to her shoulders. For them, all it takes is a brush.

Maybe she'll go home instead, and sit there in front of the television in the family room to watch Arsenio and try not to be spooked by the complex settling around her, or the fridge shutting off with a tick-tick, delaying for as long as she can having to go to bed in an empty apartment. Maybe she won't be alone, and her mom and the guy from Blockbuster will be in the bedroom fooling around, or maybe he will have already had enough of her, and she'll be at the kitchen table in front of a glass of gin when Keisha walks in, weeping over a cigarette and asking why didn't he like her, why doesn't anybody like her? Keisha will know better than to try to assure her that at least her daughter still likes her. It's not something her mother wants to hear.

Last year, some guy she met at the DMV on their third date convinced her to run away with him to California for no good reason except that neither of them had ever been there, and she stopped home while Keisha was at work long enough to pack a bag and write out a note, letting her daughter know that she'd had enough of this life and was going away to find another. She probably intended to stay on there, but she was back three weeks later, needing Keisha to pick her up at the Greyhound station because she refused to ride twenty-three hours in a car with that rat bastard. Keisha is sure that somewhere during her mother's three-week absence, certain purchases at Claire's stopped being rung in. Maybe she is saving for something because, when it comes to her mom, you just never know.

Bridget gives it up, her calls being replaced by the hum of a vacuum inside Express a few stores up ahead, one of the only places on this leg with lights still on. Keisha looks toward the top of the escalator, but Bridget isn't standing there anymore. She dumps the tape into a nearby trash can, which unfortunately has already been emptied for the evening, leaving the tape to clunk at the bottom of the new bag. She's reasonably sure Bridget doesn't see her do it or won't come digging through the trash if she did.

"You're in trouble," Gina says. "Keisha's in trouble." She sounds thrilled at the prospect, but the dimwit doesn't even know for what, probably thinks her red spill is the only thing anybody cares about, probably doesn't even know that nobody is chasing them anymore.

Far up ahead in front of the lower level of Sears at the end of the gloomy end cap, she notices someone sitting on the bench. All she can see is the silhouette. Maybe it's the Zamboni driver taking a break, except she hears the thing running somewhere upstairs. Maybe it's the pipsqueak security guard that Peggy ordered to escort the girl and her brother safely to their mom's car, or maybe it's the guy Peggy had been trying to protect them from, the one who, given a chance, will throw you into the backseat of his car and there you go.

"Circus World," Peggy says. "It's really closed." They are standing in front of the caged-over storefront that is nothing anymore but a curly-cue sign whose panels used to light up with a top-hatted ringleader on one end holding a hoop in front of him, and a tiger on the other, its tail now busted out at the end to reveal a metal frame and dormant light bulb behind it. Hanging on the cage is a piece of white cardboard that reads, 'Commercial Space For Rent' with a phone number underneath. Beyond the gate is just a stripped-down particle board shell with empty shelves still in place in case they suit the next owner, who will load them up with sneaker boxes or spring sweaters.

Peggy points toward the corner of the store. "They used to have a clown standing right there with a helium spigot coming out of his mouth and a bunch of balloons as big as beach balls tied to his hand and floating over his head. Every

94

time we came by here, Tommy would beg me for one of those goddamn balloons. The things cost about five bucks each. Then as soon as we'd walk outside, he'd immediately lose his grip on the goddamn thing, and there went my five bucks floating up into the Milky Way. He'd cry all the way home and the whole night after. Every...fucking...time."

"I remember," Keisha says. The place must've closed in the past six months, but she'd forgotten it still being here because she was so young when it mattered to her. Seeing the sign brings back a watery memory. "I used to beg my mom for one too every time we went past, but she never was fool enough to buy me one."

"I guess I was a fool," Peggy says. Her voice wilts. "I was a fool every time."

"Yeah," Keisha says, because in the pressing silence she feels she has to say something, but she's pretty sure that isn't the right thing.

Peggy recovers. "Got so I had to go out of my way to avoid walking by here so he wouldn't see them and put me through it again. Those goddamn balloons."

The three of them stand there with nothing to say to that. Somewhere, the Zamboni has gone quiet in unison.

"It's empty," Peggy says, as if it has suddenly occurred to her. "It's so dark in there. The darkest."

The recessed lights in the ceiling of the mall have dimmed further so that they cast only a mist of light over the three of them. Keisha looks beyond the fountain down the leg of the mall, past all the stores closed up for the evening or closed up for good like this one. She returns her gaze to the fountain, where the water reflects back into the toy store. On the surface of the water, she can see colors now. It's not the coins at the bottom. She knows what those colors are. The shelves are full again: Glo Worms that light up when you squeeze their middles, Teddy Ruxpins that will talk to you after your mom turns out the light for the night, Barbies who ride surf boards and drive hippie vans and have all the boys falling all over them, Slinkies that never do travel down the stairs and become a tangled snarl five minutes into playing with them, and Easy Bake Ovens that, no matter how much she begs, will never show up under the tree because one of those is liable to burn the house down. She also sees that clown still there in the front, and hovering above it, a mass of balloons, each one as big as a beach ball, sure, but when you're a kid, as big as Jupiter, so big that when you grab hold of the string, you're sure it will lift you off the ground and take you into the stratosphere, or at least someplace you've never been, far away from here.

Keisha turns to look up at Peggy's ragged face and has an indescribable urge to ask Peggy to please buy her one. Just one, and she promises to be good and finally make her bed and put away her clothes and take out the trash like she's supposed to. She'll do it all without even having to be asked. She will beg if that's what it's going to take, yank on her tangerine sleeve and whine and whine and never let up until she finally agrees.

Peggy is still looking behind her into the store, and Keisha turns to realize it hasn't changed. The shelves are still empty—no Barbies or Slinkies, no clown and no balloons. They never were big enough to lift you off the ground anyway. You think they will, but the joke's on you because the minute you lose your grip on the string, it's not you but the balloon that floats away to someplace you'll never go.

White Oaks Mall isn't long for this world. It's dying store by store, with nothing moving in to fill the empty spaces. Walk through this mall, even during business hours, and you'll find every few stores are caged over and dark inside. Keisha

96

never does look inside those empty stores as she passes by them on her way to work. There's nothing to see after all. She is looking now, though, and she is sure that she could walk the mall and stare through the bars into the darkness of what was once Radio Shack, Brown's Chicken, Illini Sporting Goods, Buster Brown Shoes, and every last store in this mall that's gone under, and she will know Peggy's right about what she said. Circus World. This place is the darkest of all.

The Girl Next Door

"I think I heard the thud when they cut his body down." I hadn't really, but I couldn't help dishing out that scrap for Susan to sink her teeth into on the other end of the line. "Of course it's weird," I said. "Having it happen on the other side of my wall. I was probably home." The living room around me was populated with gunky metal tubes, cratered where I had squeezed gobs out of them, and colored-over canvases whose scenes seemed to fade further with each passing day spent propped against my wall, unviewed by the world. I didn't even dare look at them for fear of what they'd become since yesterday. "Maybe I was painting. Maybe I could've stopped him." There were so many more maybes, but the maybes could bury you.

No sleep last night. I should've put on make-up this morning, but I hadn't felt up to it. In the shadow of the mirror, my cheeks were cavernous black holes like overused ashtrays in a bingo hall, emptied of butts but forever caked with the stubbed-out ash of a million cigarettes.

Susan asked a question, but I went on with what I was saying. "I knew him a little. He came over here maybe a dozen times. I never went over there." I went to the door and looked through the peephole. Nothing but a bubbled-out section of empty hallway. "He gave me two hundred dollars on the first day we met. He saw me staring into my empty mailbox where my financial aid cheque should've been. I mean, two weeks into the semester and I didn't have any books, was down to a couple of boxes of rice in the cupboard. We started talking in the hall, and I was telling him about my parents so far away in New Zealand, how I couldn't ask them for money because the currency exchange made it cost them double to send. That's when he offered." Another question. "No, I wasn't *hinting*. I tried to refuse. I knew he couldn't have much more money than I did, but he kept insisting, said it was hard enough not having family close by without having to worry about money on top of it. Maybe I shouldn't have taken it. Maybe he did need it."

The phone cord was stretched as far as it would go. Back in high school, Jimmy Benson blew his head off with his father's shotgun, did it inside his bedroom closet like he wanted to hold in the mess. Nobody had two words to say to Jimmy while he was clunking down the halls in overalls, boots still muddy from working on the farm, but after he was gone, suddenly everybody knew him, sharing stories about him from as far back as the third grade, some people claiming they saw it coming, while others insisting he showed no indication, but everybody competing to be the one who knew him best of all.

And here I was, latching onto every last detail and shoving it at Susan, who'd never even met him. Maybe this time I was that person who knew him best. "He used to write stories," I said. "He was so clumsy when he talked to me, couldn't put three words together without tripping over them, but his writing was different."

I plucked at a curl in my hair while, outside my window, college kids straggled by on the sidewalk, dragging along in their ratty sweats, crumpled under their hangovers, and looking no better than the lost souls who climbed out of the alleyways in the morning and sought out the dumpsters behind restaurants to see where their next meal was coming from. These were the hope for tomorrow.

99

"He had a new story every time he popped over, always wanted me to read it, waited there while I did, leaning against the wall, never daring to sit down even when I insisted.

"No, he didn't write about it. Nothing that would've... There was one about a little kid who got mad at his parents because they wouldn't let him go to a traveling carnival in town, so he ran away from home and got a job there helping cook corn dogs, and cleaning off the cars whenever somebody got sick in one. He got to eat as much junk food and ride as many rides as he wanted. It was a funny story. At the end, the parents are driving around looking for him, and they see him riding away in the front of the Ferris wheel truck. They never caught up to him."

I could remember other stories, like the guy who ran his cheating girlfriend down with his car, then waited for the other guy to leave for work, broke into his apartment, and propped her mangled corpse up onto the couch. He turned on the TV and poured her a soda from the fridge, even added ice, so she could be comfortable while she waited for her lover to get home. That's where it ended. Susan would've feasted on that one, but suddenly, I had to hold back.

"I used to hear him talking over there, when I knew he was by himself. He just talked to himself as casually as you talk to the guy next to you in class." I found the wall of my apartment—the wall I had shared with him, him on one side and me on the other—and I fell back against it, couldn't move. Susan hadn't spoken for over a minute. I didn't even know if she was still there, or if I was just spilling things to a dead line.

"Last week he came over, looking like he hadn't slept or showered in a week. He had a story for me to read, but it didn't make any sense. I kept reading, tried to figure it out, but he was standing there, watching me. I couldn't. I ended up handing it back to him, saying it was good, that I liked it. He went back to his place without saying anything. That was the last time—" The receiver dropped from my fingers and clattered against the wood floor, swiveling on the end of the unwinding cord. I left it.

He used to always fumble around trying to find something in what I painted, some detail or image from each one that spoke something to him, not like the kids in my class who pretended that they knew everything about my work, made it all about declaring their own genius by identifying the transparency in what I'd done. He just wanted to make me appreciate what I'd created, because he knew that it took more than saying it was good, more than saying you really liked it. Those were just kiss-offs, coming from people who didn't care enough to take the time to really consider it.

The painting on the easel was almost finished after over a month working on it, putting it aside, and picking it up again. It was of a girl sitting down next to a freshly-laid sidewalk, and dragging an S with her fingers through the wet concrete. He had seen it when it was only three quarters done, had been the only one yet to see it, told me it reminded him of being young and not having to worry so much about messing up, or about what other people thought of you. In a couple of days, I would take the painting to my art class where the others would tell me every stroke that was too heavy, too obvious, too vague, too tired, too scattered, or too much like the paint-by-numbers produced by assembly line hacks in the back room of the mall art store.

There were other paintings in here that I hadn't shared with anyone else. My family was too far away, and Susan was a biology major, only interested in art if it involved nude models and finding out if they ever went hard while we drew them.

101

Some of my paintings were just for him, like his stories were written only for me, the ones I had become tired of always being expected to read, wondering why he couldn't ever just come over empty-handed.

The vacancy on the other side sucked through the wall, and I could hear the crackle of the oils solidifying inside all the tubes scattered over the coffee table. The next time I squeezed one, it would produce nothing but rocks. I could see the color draining from all the canvases I'd painted over the past two years of school here. By tomorrow, the entire collection would be nothing but a whole lot of empty space.

I had hung up on Susan before getting to the point of the call. It was the money. I had received my financial aid cheque a couple of days before and had the two hundred dollars tucked in a jar in my kitchen ready to give him the next time he came over. I should've delivered it, but had just never been to his place before, figured he'd come over sooner or later.

Now what? I could find his parents at the funeral, or when they came to clean out his apartment. Should I give it to them? Did I still owe him? Did it matter?

******

He set the pencil and yellow pad onto the coffee table. It was enough for one day. He'd been at it for two straight hours now, most of the time not writing but deciding how far to go.

He stared at the last question until the words became something heavy, sinking down into a deep lake and melting away, out of sight and out of reach. The answer was the last thing to know. He could've written down something, could've finished it off any way he wanted, but he wasn't sure.

He wiped the back of his hand across his eyes as the knock came at the door. He stayed fixated on that last question. It took a second knock for him to move from his spot to open the door.

She'd never come to his door before. "My financial aid cheque finally came," she said. The first time he had ever heard her speak, he had guessed Australian, but she had quickly informed him of the difference. "I'll deposit it, and then I can pay you back."

Her fingerprints were embedded with blue paint. She'd been at it today, probably putting the finishing touches on that little girl's dress. "I told you it's no rush," he said. "I'm getting on okay."

She glanced at the legal pad on the coffee table, maybe could read from there what he'd written. Maybe he would've invited her in, would've let her read it the whole way through if she'd seemed curious. Sure he would've, had she only asked, but all she said was a quick thanks again, she really appreciated it, that he'd really saved her; before telling him she had to get back to what she was working on, was burning candles too, didn't want to burn the whole building down. One too many excuses.

She went back into her apartment, leaving him standing there. Before closing the door, he looked over her shoulder at the section of wallpaper in the hallway, the vine pattern vanishing from the sun shining on it all day through the front window. Soon all the color would be gone, an empty space among all those branches, all those leaves, and there was nothing anybody could do to stop it.

Pheochromocytoma

"That's what it is all right," Maggie says. She sits atop the examination table spread with a strip of tissue paper whose crackling beneath her always makes her question if she's really supposed to sit on it. The end of that paper, where she's mangled it and possibly infected it, will be torn free, disposed of, and replaced as soon as her time with Dr. Daniels comes to an end. "The nurse who took my blood pressure said it was up, didn't she?"

"Now Maggie—" Dr. Daniels replies.

"Didn't she?" Maggie doesn't need his affirmation. "She takes my blood pressure every time I come here, and it's always normal. That's the only symptom I wasn't sure about, but now I'm sure."

"It's probably elevated because you're getting worked up. You have to calm down about this." He's scrolling through her annotated medical history on a computer attached to an extension arm so he can wheel around the office on his stool and take his information with him. He barely manages to look her way when she comes in, always gaping at that screen, no better than anybody under thirty on the bus or the streets these days, afraid to look up from their phones for fear of missing something when all the while they're missing everything.

"At night, it feels like I swallowed a goat."

The comparison causes Dr. Daniels to look away from the computer, frowning to let her know she's exaggerating, except he never grew up with a Toggenburg named Bernie who bucked at the gate of his pen out back to escape until the latch finally gave way, Maggie's father sending her to track him to the next property half a mile away where he could undoubtedly be found gnashing up Mrs. Watt's sunflowers. When Maggie would finally corner him and secure her hand around one of his horns with Mrs. Watts crabbing from her porch for Maggie to keep that goddamn goat off her property, Bernie would hitch his head back and forth as she tried to get the rope around his neck, finally resorting to bursting forward to crash the roots of his horns into her belly just below the rib cage. That's exactly how it feels now, forty years later—Bernie and her father long gone from this earth—a force as hard as horn and skull, enough to knock her over, only now Bernie is ramming her from the inside and can buck and buck, but will never get free. "It's worst at night."

"What else is there?" He has abandoned his searching through her history to gape at the chart of lungs on the wall, the insides filled with pink bulbs and arrows swooping around to show the paths of air coming and going.

"Cramps, especially in my legs." Though the real pain isn't due for hours, she kneads one thigh with her fingers like she did the night before, the polyester leg of her Ben Franklin uniform scratching the skin underneath. The inky veins squiggle across the carved-out bones of her hand in a way that makes her have to look away, examining the lungs herself, though that isn't her problem. Where is the hand that decades ago clasped Jerry Tuttle's as they walked along Callhoun Road after ditching Spanish class together? She had never before skipped a class, rarely even stayed home sick because that just meant more time for chores, but was so easily convinced by Jerry's insistence that they couldn't possibly sit in class when the sun was shining so brightly outside. On the walk home, when she wasn't looking at those sideburns that informed the world Jerry didn't live by their rules, she stared at her own hand swinging between them because simply feeling his hand there in hers, feeling his tender fingers and leaky palm, wasn't, and could never be, enough.

"But last night it felt like every muscle was pulling at once." She goes on without him prompting her. "And my skin is like a sheet. I looked in the mirror and thought I was dead, and I couldn't stop sweating, and my heart was beating out of my chest. It's everything they list. It couldn't be anything else. I can barely make it through work. David, my manager, complained I was freaking out the customers."

"It could be a lot of things. You have to be careful with the internet." This coming from a guy she's seen punching in her symptoms on his computer to find out what he's dealing with and what medications work best, learning to be a doctor as he goes along. Maybe he should look up something about bedside manner. "You can punch in any symptom and find a hundred conditions associated with it," he says. "And anybody who can make a website has a diagnosis. These days everyone's some kind of medical expert. You have to be careful buying into it. It could send you over the edge."

"I didn't find this on the internet. I don't even have a computer. I read it in a book." She has the book right in her purse, *Differential Diagnosis,* but thinks better of producing it. She chose it from the box marked 'Free' out in front of the World's Bookstore mostly because its obnoxious lime-green cover caught her eye. It was happenstance, and what if she hadn't noticed it, hadn't walked by that store on her way to get coffee, because for once she didn't want to sit alone out back in the concrete-walled break room that always makes her feel like she is waiting for some cop to enter to start an interrogation, sometimes wishing that were the case so at least she wouldn't have to drink her coffee alone. What if she threw the book into her closet, another free thing that in the end isn't worth anything, and never stumbled onto what was inside her? Who would've ever known? Certainly not Dr. Daniels here. The sweat running down the inside of one arm sends a tremor through her.

"There are tests." He is back to looking at the computer. "But you were in not six months ago, and we ran blood, urine, and even an MRI, though I didn't think it was warranted. I just thought it might put your mind at ease. Sometimes that's all it takes. I don't think the insurance company would approve another round of them. These things don't just pop up overnight. We would've noticed something irregular back then."

"Don't bother. I don't need a test. It's right there, on the adrenal gland." She presses her fingers down into her abdomen until she feels a knot there, producing a peristalsis that runs from her pelvis up her throat to her tongue, where she clamps her mouth closed and gulps back the nausea.

"Have you slept at all lately, Maggie?" He leans close, but keeps his hand cupped around his mouse.

One more swallow just to be sure. "Insomnia. That's part of it. Who could sleep with the cramps and the pain? And knowing all the while it's growing."

"I could prescribe something for that. Not getting enough sleep will bring on any number of problems." He is already typing it into his computer to whoosh it off to her pharmacy of choice. Problem solved.

"I've taken those pills. All they do is cover up what's really wrong. You just want me to forget what I have. There's no pill going to fix this. I need surgery to get it out. *Now.*"

Bernie comes at her again, driving his horns through her belly, dividing her flesh, but stalling at her spine, folding her over onto herself and pushing her vertebrae out in a hunchback. She vaults forward on the table, nearly leaping off, the paper underneath her crackling with the same sound it had on Christmas morning so long ago, and she slides her hands underneath it like she did the flaps of tissue paper within that clothing box so big she could barely hold it on her lap. She knew by the size and density of that box that it was a coat before she even removed the lid—knew which one too because she had shown her daddy the Nil's white Penny Down coat, had slipped it on while with him at the Peppermill indoor mall 10 miles away from their house during one of their infrequent trips into town. She had swiveled in front of the three-piece mirror, and swanked across the floor for him so he could see just how fresh she looked in it, just so there could be no doubt in his mind which one she wanted to replace the thread-bare parka she had worn at least one winter too many. He even scooped back her bangs from in front of her face and said she looked really pretty in it, so much like her mother that he could hardly believe it.

When she saw that box, she thought for sure he'd gotten it for her, but she should've known better after seeing her only other Christmas present: a pair of clunky tan Caterpillar work boots that promised to wear like tree stumps on her feet, but would also be something she'd grudgingly appreciate when every puddle in the field no longer drained through the cracks of the ancient leather pair she had been living with for too long. She should've known that the clothing box was just a little too dense to contain the fluffy white jacket that he had told her would never be practical with all the work she had to do around the farm, even though she assured him

108

that she would wear her old parka for nasty jobs, be extra careful when she did wear it doing everything else, and clean off anything she got on it before it could even dry. When she pulled away the tissue paper, it should've been no shock to find a Carhart winter construction work coat that would be so much warmer than the Penny Down coat she had requested and be as durable as tire tread, but would also guarantee her slot among the select group of farm boys who started their day at least two hours before everyone else, arriving to school with wind-chapped faces, mud-streaked hands, bags beneath their eyes, and pig shit rimming the souls of their boots, which promised to keep everyone as far away as possible.

A hand falls onto her back. "Maggie, did it happen again?"

"Yes, usually it's only at night, but it must be getting worse. It needs to come out." She slowly sits up straight, shedding his hand, and rattling the paper again like she had when she'd folded the tissue paper back over the coat that she knew would keep Jerry Tuttle from ever asking her to skip Spanish again. She wouldn't have skipped Spanish again anyway, not after the first time telling her dad why she was kept after school and lost an hour of daylight, her confession bringing silence to the house the two of them shared since her mother died of lung cancer years before. Only the slither of his belt could be heard, slipping free of its loops, and outside the wind hushing across their ten acres and shuddering against their loose windows. She might look out any one of those windows for as far as she could, and not see another house except the one belonging to Mrs. Watts, who would promptly shut the curtains and pretend to be elsewhere if Maggie ever banged on the door. No other houses out there and aside from the animals in the barn, not another living soul.

Dr. Daniels sits back on his stool, but seems leery of taking his eyes off her. "Just take the pills. Let's get you rested. You couldn't undergo surgery in this condition anyway. Let's just wait on it, okay?" She doesn't miss his eyes flicking toward the clock in the corner of the screen.

She slides off the table and slips past Dr. Daniels out the door, hearing her name as she makes her way to the waiting room, dodging a guy in his forties being led by a nurse to an examining room where he will undoubtedly receive a clean bill of health after already providing them with his insurance information, because somebody needs to pay for the delivery of all this useless information.

Her legs begin to seethe as she steps up onto the bus, and the college kid driving sees something in her face that compels him to ask her if she's okay, reaches out to help her up the last step. He's better at acting concerned than Dr. Daniels. On the ride home, a mother with her two kids riding next to her in the seat ahead of Maggie keeps glancing back to evaluate the woman huffing breaths in and out, either willing Maggie to shut up or deciding if she needs the Heimlich or something.

Her belly is churning by the time she walks the two blocks and arrives at her first-floor apartment. The dwindling sun floats in a haze through her patio door on the plains of airborne dust. The wall surrounding her patio blocks out most of the light, along with any kind of view aside from the tips of the swing sets in the neighboring daycare center, the shouts of play that usually sprinkle into her boxy living room gone quiet for the day. The approaching evening drags like funeral gowns from every protruding piece of furnishing, decolorizing the print hanging on the wall over the couch of Van Gogh's 'Cypresses' that she used her 33% Ben Franklin discount to custom frame. In this light, the fields turn to concrete, the sky to slate, and the cypress to a raven's wing.

The red light on her phone blinks once, and she punches the button, switching on the lamp as she does, but only producing a basketball of light against the enormity of the dusk.

"Hey Mag, it's Gal." After Gal sees her seven- and ten-year-olds off to school each morning, she works the register at Ben Franklin until she's due to meet them coming off the bus. She was working 3 today, next to Maggie on 2. Three months before, Gal, her kids visiting grandma for the weekend, asked Maggie to grab a drink after work, but after Maggie's insistence on having to go home without any particular reason she could come up with, Gal hasn't asked again, maybe just hasn't been free of her kids since. They still chat between customers, but Gal's never called here, shouldn't even have the number.

Gal explains how after Maggie left early, they got slammed, and Dave had to hop on a register to get the cattle through, something he never does while running the show in the day, and the main reason he applied for assistant manager in the first place, to avoid customer interaction at all cost.

"He got really pissed off about it," she says. "I wouldn't think about calling in sick tomorrow." She leaves it at that. Dave pissed. That's nothing new. He's attending community college to get his degree in communications and is sure he's going to be some hotshot, on-location TV announcer for the local station when he finally gets his degree and can tell Ben Franklin Crafts to kiss his ass. He'd have canned Maggie long ago if she weren't so in with the owner, had already known him a decade when seven years ago Dave, just sixteen, turned in his first applications to every place in town, praying for anybody to give him a chance. Now, he wants to recreate Ben Franklin in his own vision with a young, vital, fun staff. The young always think things would be so much better if nobody old was around, never can seem to recognize where they and everyone else are headed eventually.

Maggie retrieves the green book from her purse and drops it on the coffee table next to a hardcover of *Gray's Anatomy* and a crumb-covered plate on which she'd had toast that morning. Maybe she will check through it one more time, make sure she isn't wrong. She's been through it a dozen times already, though. Nothing else matches so precisely.

She spent last night tumbling in sheets soaked cold with her sweat, glued to her and then peeling off, as she tried to find the perfect position to quiet the yanking in her thighs and the battering in her belly, all while not inhibiting the stampede in her chest which might stop cold if she didn't allow it the necessary room to run.

The only thing that got her through to morning was promising herself it was the last night of this, that when she told Dr. Daniels, he would promptly cut it out of her. He never will, though. How can he know what's wrong with her body when he doesn't even examine it, lets her sit on that table and tell him all about it while he nods and sighs and wonders if he's yet displayed enough concern to show her the door? She can get a different doctor, but he'll say the same thing, probably won't even agree to see her if the insurance has given up on her.

Bernie butts her just to make sure she doesn't forget him. He was at it the whole way home. He wants out. *"Just take the pills, Maggie."* She mimics his exasperation, but her attempt falls dead in the room like a desperate comedy routine that some sap has only ever tried in front of his mirror or his mother, both of whom howled and assured him soon enough he'd be able to quit his mail carrier's job to make people laugh full-time.

Maybe Dr. Daniels has a point, though. She has the old prescription somewhere below the sink. Maybe if she only gets some sleep and gets a handle on things, he will open her up and see how wrong he was.

She goes to the bathroom, flipping on the light to see in the mirror how the passing years have trampled over her, the brown in her curls gone to lead, her cheeks withering peaches sinking into themselves, and her eyes slithering beneath the plastic lenses like pebbles at the bottom of a stream. The closest thing she wears to make-up is the Chapstick coating her lips in wax, and her only jewelry is a beaded chain, wrapped around her neck and attached to those clunky frames to prevent them from shattering to the earth and leaving her a squinting mole trying to find her way around.

She recognizes herself like never before: the woman who dodders along the sidewalk oblivious to the people glaring as they dart around her with someplace important to go; the woman who carries on a conversation with herself at the grocery about what to make for dinner, unaware of the strange looks she's getting from all the passersby; the woman who buys one scratch ticket each week, positive each time that this will be the week she'll hit the jackpot, but never quite sure which ticket she should choose, deaf to the line of sighs and grumbles behind her as she stands at the counter and points from one to the other and then back again.

God, she used to hate those women. A cramp seizes her thigh and releases, sending her against the open door and slamming the knob into the wall. Bernie spears her for good measure, and she gladly drops to her knees, away from the vision of herself that couldn't be true.

113

When had she stopped wearing make-up? She sure remembers when she started—about the same time she received that coat, and needed some color to offset the brown shell that had consumed her. She would hunch down in the seat as soon as the bus pulled away from her stop, staring into her oyster-shaped compact and caring so much who stared back at her, painting over her chapped lips, powdering over her freckled Opie cheeks, and lining black sludge along her eyes to sharpen the corners into stingers. Jerry noticed the change, but instead of asking her to skip Spanish again, he offered her a ride home in his car, dropping her off where her bus was supposed to so she could walk down the road and into her driveway like any other afternoon. Unbeknownst to her father, that was how she began getting home every afternoon for over a month, until that one afternoon Jerry drove her to one of the subdivisions not too far from school, and up to the split-level that was his house. That was the day he took Maggie away forever.

From her knees, she opens the cabinet beneath the sink. The pain comes again, not blunt this time, but searing, not the root of the horn, but the tip sinking into her. She latches onto the cabinet, feeling the top hinge give enough that it will never close right again. She claws out the package of toilet paper, the three remaining rolls tumbling from the plastic onto the floor around her feet. Her fingers fumble through a tangled strip of gauze and over crust-covered bottles, shoving them out and spilling something goopy onto the floor. The wet coolness of it finds its way into her ancient leather shoes like the rainwater in the fields so long ago.

She'd been over two hours late that night by the time Jerry finally dropped her off, well after the day was shot, and her father stood in the living room fresh, from out back, unshaven from the morning, work pants doubly soiled from doing both their shares, his features shading as the sun descended on the day. He didn't say anything to her, just stared until she answered the question unasked. "I was just with a boy from school."

He didn't respond, his only movement a dirty hand reaching to grasp the back of the rocking chair in front him, his fingers compressing in a fist around a spindle as the silence expanded between them and reached critical mass. "We just went over to his house for a while." Still nothing, and the silence came again with the compelling need to fill it. The rest came out piece by piece, his face sometimes tilting ever so slightly at points when he knew she was holding back. She inevitably told him more than he needed to know, right down to them doing it on Jerry's parent's bed. Anything to keep the silence at bay. She should've told him how Jerry had asked her more than once if she really wanted to, helped her trembling fingers with every button, ran his fingertips across her body with no more pressure than the touch of a summer breeze, and molded himself around her after it was over to make sure she knew she wasn't alone. His arm wrapped over her body was the only thing keeping her from crying into his parents' lilac-smelling sheets for no reason she could discern, except maybe the dawning realization that he had taken her so far away from where she had existed every other day of her life. He left her to wonder whether coming home with him was the best thing or worst thing she'd ever done. The longer he held her, the more she knew the answer, would've told her dad that it wasn't having sex with him but lying together afterward that had delayed her so much. That was the part she remembered most, the part that meant everything. She eventually just said, "He really cares about me," but she wasn't even sure of that herself.

Her father broke his silence. "He does, huh?" He nodded as he said it. "I bet he loves you. Because he knows he hooked himself a sure thing, some gal willing to come over anytime his parents are away." His voice was a fifth of whiskey and 200,000 cigarettes later. He and his wife, two chimneys in love. He had quit after she died, but the stink still oozed out of his clothes, could never be completely expelled from the pockets of the house, and never could he manage to cough up all that gravel left over in his lungs. Maggie knew he had since been sneaking them now and again too, when he was stuck awake in the middle of the night remembering his wife with glass in hand, or when things got so tight with the bills coming in that trying to hold onto the farm felt like carrying a Buick on his back. He probably had a dozen sticks while waiting for her to show that afternoon. "Guess that's what I got for a daughter now. A goddamn sure thing."

She wasn't really sure if he was telling her or asking her, but she shook her head just the same. He dug a hand in his back pocket and pulled out a flat bottle half gone. Must've taken it into the fields with him. He sloshed it back in his throat and went on. "But I guess I knew that all along. Now come on over here."

"Why?" She'd never talked back to him before, had always just gone forward and accepted the belt, but something about him tonight made her ask.

"Just do what I say." His voice fell off, as if he'd run out of air before he could finish saying it. He must've forgotten to breathe in between words.

She remained by the window and glanced out, but beyond the pane was nothing but open land, with only one road cutting through it that was only ever traveled by them or Tom Douger, who lived alone a couple of miles down and was

116

too old to drive at this time of night, too old to be good for much of anything anymore. She started toward him, knew better than to refuse, and he reached for that belt, unbuckled it and pulled it free from the loops—but that night, he didn't use it on her backside, slung it instead over the back of the chair where his fist had just been, and there it stayed until morning.

She looks straight down between her bent thighs at the rolls of toilet paper melting into a puddle of silky brown liquid. A bolt hits her, and her legs pinch together. Not tonight. She fumbles into the cabinet below the sink for the pills, but in the darkness retrieves an artifact, a Gillette double-edged Knack safety razor her dad every morning dragged down the flaps of his cheeks, curved along his jawbone, and chipped at the strip under his nose. For some reason, she'd included it with the small box of items she claimed from his pigsty of an apartment following the stroke that took him five years ago, 20 years after he lost the farm trying to work it himself. Back here, using the old blade, still petrified with cream from the last time he shaved his face, she ran it along her legs, achieving the closest shave she'd ever had, but in the process turning her calves into a crime scene. She bought a new box of blades, but instead of throwing out the used one, had tossed it into the top bathroom drawer where each time she retrieved her hairbrush, she eyed its body there at the bottom, melting into rust, and cautiously avoided catching her fingers on either of the two edges.

She continued to use the Knack razor for another month with improving skill, though still hacking herself at least a couple of times each go round, causing the insurance guy she was seeing at the time to joke that she needed to stop walking through the rose bushes. She went back to the Bic, ten-to-a-bag, pink plastic disposables soon after, but it's been a couple of weeks since she's found the energy to even use one of them, not that anybody nowadays is running his fingers over her calves, or even getting a peek at them. Not even Dr. Daniels disrobes her anymore.

She rotates the bottom of the shaft, and the top of her father's old razor hinges open like the electronic glass doors at the grocery store. The double-sided blade she removes is corroded along both edges from disuse. She gets herself to her feet, her shoes slipping in the spill and her thighs knotting up into fists. Her reflection melts around the edges as her vision fails, and she stops looking before she loses it altogether. The muck on the blade remains stuck under the water from the faucet, forcing her to slide a nail along the metal to remove it, the edge catching her across the pad of her thumb. She shuts off the water and pops the thumb into her mouth like a sucker. Sharp enough.

She sets herself down on the toilet as another burst comes from her belly, like somebody shoving a broomstick down into the hollows of her pelvis. Her throat emits a moan as the stick burrows through her organs, knocking them aside. The blade quivers in her fingers, nearly dropping and being lost forever. She sets it delicately on the edge of the sink as the pain subsides, knowing another bout is not far behind. She unbuttons her pants and strips them down to her knees, leaving herself naked from belly button to knees, a hash of blood appearing on the inner waistband of her pants from her sliced thumb. The single hand towel hangs off-kilter from the bar, smudged with something that looks like the mustard she slathered on last night's dinner of microwaved hot dogs. She needs to throw the whole set of towels in the wash, should be washing her towels and sheets every week whether they look

118

like they need it or not. Who knows what's growing or burrowing in that thick fabric?

She positions the blade between two fingers and watches as the flesh of her belly palpitates. It's not Bernie in there, but something that breathes separate from her, will grow and steal from her to live, steal until it steals more than she can give. Her legs stretch out in a narrow V in front of her, the waistband of her pants shackling her knees, and her shoes punch against the wall in front of her. One more night, and maybe it won't be so bad, not this bad. Then the thing hits her hard enough to squirt vomit up onto the back of her tongue.

She closes her eyes and runs the razor three inches straight down rib to navel, but when she looks, it's left nothing but a coarse white line like the scratch of a fingernail. "Get rid of it," she says. She should've ordered Dr. Daniels to do so back at the office, should've refused to leave until he did.

After that night her father had deemed her a sure thing, he couldn't stay away. For too long he'd been biding the isolation of not having his wife anymore, trying to sweat it out during the long days of work, and drinking it away during his nights like a dark curtain drawn around his memory. Maggie supposes she made him feel something again, as her pleas, shouts, and struggles relented to silence, tears, and rigidity, some kind of comfort from being close to another person in the darkness, the bourbon that let him forget who it was, nothing more than a dream to take him through until the sun rose again with a crashing headache, and the brutal line of tasks awaiting them, with no time to speak or even look at each other, both holding onto the belief that it had never happened, or at least never would again, that tonight would be back to normal, them resuming being just a father and a daughter again.

She brings the razor back to the start and this time pushes the corner of it downward, denting the skin, pushing deeper and then piercing it. She keeps her eyes open and draws it downward by inches, a pink agitated fissure appearing behind it and the blood surfacing in the fold like spilled ink, pink stained to black, the blade occasionally slipping free from the path so she has to back up, find it again, and continue on. It feels and looks like nothing more than a line drawn down her belly with a red ball-point pen, but by the time she gets to the bottom, the top has started to ribbon over the side.

She'd let Jerry invite her over one more time after the first, but this time the tears did come, so many they had to change his parents' sheets afterward, and when he tried to comfort her by wrapping his arm around her, she shrugged it off and curled into herself until he told her they really needed to get her home. Never again would she see the inside of his house or even look his way in Spanish class. He knew his sure thing was over, but a few weeks later he did step up to his responsibility without questioning the decision she made for the both of them, just grateful to be off the hook. She expected nothing except for him to skip school to drive her, give her a hundred and seventy bucks that nobody in his family would even miss, and wait outside in the parking lot for it to be over so they could commence forgetting they'd ever even known each other.

Inside the frigid room, cowering within her gown atop the vinyl examining table, she told the doctor flat out, "Get it out of me." He'd paused there and looked at her as if he'd never met a girl before who'd requested such an atrocity be done to her, and him never before having to perform it. For an instant, he didn't look like he could. He did, though. Dr.

120

Flores. He was a doctor who knew when his patient was really sick.

"Close," she says. The word sheds spittle from her lips. "Very close. I promise." She isn't through yet, though, and begins to cut the line once more, pushing blood out from the seam. Her forehead feels like cold mayonnaise. She swallows over and over, but her mouth is always full, saliva slopping over molars like waves hitting the sea wall. A single trickle of sweat courses down her cheek and plops onto her hip. She travels the entire three inches, and the air sizzles in the wound, devouring all her body's other complaints. She controls it now. No damn sleeping pills needed.

The razor leaves her fingers, falls flat on the side of her belly, but with a shiver of her body, it rattles to the floor. She'll need to find it again. Blood filters through her ashen pubic hair, strings down her thighs, and plinks into the toilet water below. She's always wondered if Doctor Flores missed something in her back then, because as she climbed into Jerry's car, she felt it heavy in her and continued to feel it as she stared straight ahead during the interminable ride home, has felt that something left behind, and carried it with her all these years.

She reaches down to try to find the blade, but she can't look down, and her fingers don't even hit the floor. It's an impossible search. She remembers something, though, opens the drawer next to her and dabs her fingers around the bottom until she finds it, sliding her fingernails underneath to pry it loose from its fusion to the wood. It's a miracle that she retrieves it without cutting off a finger, but she comes out with the blade her father had left for her in the Knack razor before the vessel in his brain exploded.

Whatever it is inside her is buried deep. It's no wonder Dr. Flores couldn't reach it with his hooked scraper, nor Dr.

Daniels with his urine tests and MRIs, but there's no hiding now. With enough swipes of her father's razor, she'll get there eventually.

About Her Face

I - The Dancer

The canary-yellow Backyard Safari binoculars that Liam bought his son Ryan to watch birds in the back yard, or play Russian Spy with his buddies between the neighborhood houses, are now pressed to Liam's glasses as he gazes out through the paneled windows of his garage door. He's trained on the second floor window across the street where the tie-dyed bodice, cut at the waist by the sill and decapitated by the quarter drawn shade, swivels and charges and retreats and arches and slumps and roils and stalls with such possession that Liam, from his place atop the seat of his riding lawn mower in his closed-up garage, has no doubt in his mind that he is hearing the music she is dancing to, note for note.

With the sun already sinking beneath the next block, the space inside the garage looks like it's hanging with soot from a recently extinguished fire. He keeps his eye on her window, and sucks on the one-hit that was painted to resemble a cigarette thirty years ago when he bought it off a buddy in high school, the perfect disguise from cops passing in their cars as he and Kylie passed it back and forth while hoofing it home from school on Realy Road to the neighborhood where they both lived. They were still too young to be smoking cigarettes back then, but nobody was going to lay down the law on them for that. Now, the thing has been scarred so many times over

123

the years from being stashed in the nearest tight place, or dropped by lazy fingers while hastily trying to slip it into his pocket. Most of the white paint and brown filter are scratched away. It isn't going to fool anybody, least of all his wife, Wendy, who remembers how he was when she first met him, and knows that even 18 years of marriage and two kids later, he hasn't changed much. If she sees a burning ember in front of his face, it is no cigarette.

Kylie was never his girlfriend, but sometimes if he got her high enough, she would invite him inside before her mom got home from work, letting him make out with her and sneak a hand up her shirt to play around. He can still remember the double-hook clasp of her bra that took him so long to unfasten between pinching and yanking fingers that by the time he did, long gone was her buzz and her willingness. Eventually, he just resorted to burrowing a hand underneath the cup to claw at her nipples, until she hurled him off and told him enough already, her mom would whoop his ass if she found him here feeling up her daughter. His fingers involuntarily form a scoop in the air in front of him as he wonders if now he could've slipped open that clasp like a gigolo and touched her the way she wanted to be touched, touched her so she couldn't help but let him go further, as far as he wanted and damn her mother coming home. Last he heard, Kylie had married a fisherman she met after going to college on the east coast. She stayed out there with him, never moved back. Liam doesn't know if it worked out.

He inhales, and the weed he procured from a kid named Hutch, who works with him behind Marsh's deli counter, pops and cracks. Goddamn seeds. He could plant a field out back with all the ones in this quarter.

The binoculars magnify things about as much as cupping your hands around your eyes and looking through the tunnels of your fingers. In the window across the street, she's stopped dancing and is stooped over an unseen stereo next to her, adjusting the music, letting him see nothing but a sack of pulled up hair that's collapsed to the side from all the gyrations, exposing beneath it only the smooth curve of her jawline.

He's fallen in the habit of watching the women passing his counter during lags at the grocery store, but when one rolls her cart past without looking his way, allowing him only a view of her partial profile or streaming head of hair, he will often emerge from behind the window of sliced meat and casually trail behind her, straightening the meat coolers as he goes, official Marsh business in his white butcher's scrubs, until she turns the right way to give him a full look at her face. That's all he needs, whether beauty or beast, to release him from the curiosity and allow him to return to the deli counter, where, undoubtedly, a string of impatient mothers have accumulated with numbers clamped in their fists and children tugging at their legs to come on, the mothers huffing at having to wait an eternity to purchase nitrite-ridden meat that would probably give their kids cancer if they actually ate their lunches once in a while.

A couple of weeks ago, Liam followed a woman with flowing black Asian-looking hair down four aisles at Marsh as she remained married to the shelves, shifting her focus from them to her list and back again, her hair always safely shielding her face, and when she finally sensed his presence behind her as she chose a checkout lane, she whirled around on him. He grabbed for the nearest thing, a bag of chocolate Cadbury Eggs, and pretended to right it among the dozens of others as he examined her, sure she must've been intentionally concealing some grotesque birthmark or horrible disfigurement the whole time, shocked to see just a face there—not too pretty, not too homely, just plain—not even Asian, certainly nothing bizarre or hideous enough to follow her halfway around the store to see.

He slides off the seat of the lawn mower and out the side door of the garage into the yard. He makes his way to the front, the coming night chill snapping away any vague feeling of a buzz that Hutch's ditch weed provided. Twenty more one-hits and he might just shed the headache leftover from inhaling nitrites all day.

In the window, she gets her sound system working again and is back at it, using that section of floor next to the bed for all it's worth, but still not giving him enough. Sometimes he just needs to see a face. He can't believe that in the three weeks since they moved into the neighborhood, he has never seen her. With his ever-changing shift at the deli, opening Sunday mornings, closing Mondays, working midday Thursday, it seems that one of those times, he should've seen her coming or going.

He has only ever met her actuarial scientist husband— Jeff, Liam thinks his name is—in the driveway while Liam was dragging his city bags out to the curb for Tuesday morning pick-up, and Jeff was cutting down the mailbox of the previous owner. The mailbox was fashioned by Harry Sully into a three-foot-tall wooden S that was supposed to be a monument to his last name, but the support post running up through the middle of it made it instead resemble a giant dollar sign. Liam and Wendy had endured two straight days of listening to the grinding of Harry Sully's bandsaw, intermingled with bouts of swearing coming from his garage as he put the thing together. Jeff took it down with a 30-second brattle of his chainsaw, shaking his head as it sat there on his lawn like the carcass of a gopher that had been tunneling all through his lawn for weeks before he finally hunted it down. Jeff mentioned his wife's name in the brief conversation in which he described that mailbox as a monstrosity, but Liam can't remember it now, wonders what she does with herself while Jeff is away all day, crunching statistics and calculating the probability of someone's stepping off the curb to be hit by a bus, or his house being crushed by a meteor that's been traveling toward earth for the last billion years.

Liam takes cover next to the garage behind the Butterfly bush, and pushes the Safari binoculars through the branches, but from this angle, her dance floor is blocked by the two-story birdhouse suspended just left of the window on a sixteen-foot-tall pole. It's another one of Harry's woodworking creations, with a genuine shingled roof and at least twelve holes cut into it with a perch outside each one, waiting for a flock of birds to take up residence that will never come. When Jeff realizes that no bird ever lands on it, he's bound to take his chainsaw to that too.

Taking a hit as he goes, Liam rounds the bush and crosses his front lawn. He scans the short street which contains only six other houses aside from these two. No cars are coming, and nobody is outside retrieving the mail or getting something out of their car.

He crosses into the middle of his front yard, the dusk falling like mosquito netting over him, keeping him relatively obscured from any passerby. The night is coming on later now, in another week daylight savings, and the streets filled with kids thinking that daylight means they need never go to bed. There will be no standing on the lawn to get a better look at things then.

He glances back at his house, but neither of his kids are gawking at him from the windows. The downstairs light is undoubtedly Ryan playing Minecraft in the family room, and the upstairs light must be Miranda checking the Facebook account they'd just agreed to let her open, though she is too young, so she can explore other worlds on the computer and have as much fun as her friends seem to. Maybe he should worry about the two of them. He's tried to play Ryan's game, but it plays like all he's doing is moving croutons around. Miranda has a password on her Dell which he should demand access to, but hasn't, so he can't find out what's so damn interesting there. He's lucky to get a grunted *Hey Dad* from either of them while they have their heads buried in the screens, and usually that much takes him nudging them on the shoulder to bring them back to reality.

After one last look around, he peers through the binoculars at her window straight on. The twenty or so feet he's advanced affords him a view of the bottom half of her face when she turns just right, a glimpse of her blunt, hefty nose and lips that he can see moving as she sings to whatever song she's grooving to. He sucks in, but the hit has gone cold, and all he gets is a chilly whistle of March wind. She twirls on him, and he is back to looking at her ball of hair that, when unclipped, must trickle down on her shoulders with the tenderness of dropping leaves in October. He can almost imagine it being Kylie up there with her hair clipped back, not for dancing but for soccer, and those legs built like no other girl's he'd ever seen from her booting around that ball every chance she got. Kylie would've made that tie-dye herself in her bathtub, and the music playing would have been Duran Duran or Depeche Mode.

The picture keeps blurring over from trying to look through his bifocals, so he presses the binoculars hard into his eyes, the glass frames crushing against his forehead. It focuses the picture for a moment, and then she and everything in her room suddenly wash to white. He removes the binoculars to see Wendy's car pulling into the driveway. He lets the one-hit drop from his lips into the grass, but the binoculars tangle around his neck, and she is out of the car before he can remove them.

"What are you doing out here?" She's wearing a blouse and skirt from her day at the Filene's make-up counter. He always marvels at how they make her dress up so much for a job that barely pays more than he makes slinging meat. "And what are you doing with those?"

"Just—" Her hair is as big as an Indian headdress, and all the hairspray she blasted on it that morning has, eight hours later, caramelized into something brittle enough to shatter if you ran your fingers through it. Her face is electric, charged with a carpet of pink rouge on her cheeks and her lips coated in some color as dark as asphalt sealant. They are going broke keeping her in clothes, hair spray, and clown makeup, all so she can spend her days spritzing every passing gal with perfume, or running a lipstick across her hand and promising that with the proper color tone, she can be one of the beautiful people.

He finds his explanation as she waits within the open car door. "Just picking up the yard. I found these." He finally slips his head free from the binoculars' strap.

"Where are the kids?" She acts as if she found him on a bar stool down the street, thinks that just because she comes home smelling like Dolce & Gabbana instead of turkey and bologna, that she occupies a higher place in this world.

"Inside."

129

"I hope you didn't just leave Miranda on the computer. You don't know what kids do to other kids on those things. She doesn't understand. She needs time limits, and you've got to watch her."

He glances up at the window across the street, but she's gone, the room dark. Maybe she was scared by the car lights, maybe is right then looking out at Liam getting chastised by his wife and wondering what percentage of man he is.

Wendy glances back down the driveway and across the street. Even in the dwindling light, she seems to register every flick of his eye. That's probably why he saves his appraisal of strange women for when he is safely at work. "You were just picking up out here? The kids haven't been outside for two months. What needed picking up?"

"I just noticed them when I was going in. They must've been buried under the snow all winter."

"If you wanted to pick up, you should've started in the living room. Did you tell Ryan to do something with his volcano on the coffee table?" Liam and Ryan had constructed a volcano out of chicken wire and Plaster of Paris for his science project at school. Although the baking soda and red-colored vinegar gurgled up from the middle and flowed down the sides in red frothy streams that looked enough like real lava to dazzle nine-year-olds, Mrs. Carr had seen this experiment done too many times to be impressed, had even strongly dissuaded her students beforehand from choosing certain overdone experiments such as that one, which Ryan took instead as a suggestion. Four or five days ago, Ryan hauled the thing home and left it on the coffee table with a C+ tag attached to the bottom, and that's where it has sat since, forcing Liam to sit up instead of slouch down in his chair in order to see the TV in the evenings, and hold his Schlitz in hand instead of setting it down, undoubtedly causing him to drink double what he would normally, what with having the can always so close to his mouth.

"I told him," Liam says. He had too, but that was three or four days ago, and the volcano surely still sits like a giant desert ant hill in the middle of their living room.

"I bet he listened too." She glances at him and then across the street again where the light is still off upstairs, but there is nothing of any peculiarity visible. She hesitates as if considering any number of questions to shoot at him, because she knows something about this isn't right, but instead she lets out an exhale from the deepest recesses of her lungs that sounds like she's been holding it in the entire day, while clenching her teeth in a smile and telling every ugly bag who came up to the counter that with the right eyeliner and a little lipstick, she can be nothing short of Cleopatra, Queen of the Nile. "Those things are probably ruined now after sitting out all winter. The kids got to start taking care of their stuff, or I'm going to stop buying them anything."

He stands there as he tries to follow what she's referring to. The volcano? Maybe Hutch's herb is just a slow starter because Liam feels it beginning to make itself known in his temples like pinwheels whorling in a gusty wind.

"The binoculars," she says.

He could've assured her that aside from being too weak to make out whether or not the woman across the street showed cleavage above the V-neck of her tie-dye T-shirt, the binoculars work just fine. He also could've told her that no matter how many presents their kids ruin or don't appreciate, she won't stop burying them on Christmas and on their birthdays. She can't help herself, heaping so many packages on them that the kids even seem a little bored by the end from unwrapping so much, paralyzed by all the choices to play with after the pile of loot and mangled paper sits in front of them like a plaster volcano you just don't know what to do with anymore, all of the presents making you no happier than a C+. As Liam watches them unwrapping, he inevitably feels a rising toxin inside him, blood-red vinegar overflowing the edges as he wonders how far she has carved into their credit cards this year and will they ever come out from under again? Certainly not with her commission on compacts and lipsticks or his thirty-five hours a week behind the deli counter, not even with his share of the family furniture store that he doesn't need to do anything to earn except collect a cheque every month. That cheque doesn't make them rich, at least not until his parents will the whole place to him, but it makes Wendy think they are. His share in Upton Furnishings with its three floors of inventory may be the sole reason she married him, a hope for a future bonanza that may not come quick enough to save them and probably won't be around very long when it does. What the hell does he know about running a furniture store?

Wendy heads up the driveway, but topples into the side panel of the car as if one of her high heels has turned over on her. She grapples for a handhold on the grooves of the hood, remaining stooped there on buckled knees like somebody in church stooping forward after communion to show the altar the sign of peace.

He starts toward her, but she sees him in her periphery and slaps up a hand to keep him back. It isn't her heel. Six months ago, she went to the doctor after feeling weak and tingly in her legs, and after giving her an MRI and examining the fluid from her spine, he determined she was in the early stages of MS. She came home that day spouting off that Dr. Bellamy didn't know his ass from his elbow, and there was no way she was buying his knee-jerk diagnosis without a second opinion. Six months later, and she has yet to seek out that second opinion, and as far as the tingling in her legs, her fatigue, and her worsening vision for which she won't get glasses and probably shouldn't be driving, she and Liam just don't talk about it.

Latching onto the edge of the hood, she scales up the side of the car to get her legs underneath her, presses her skirt flat against her thighs, takes that breath in again that she had been holding all day, and proceeds up the driveway into the house.

Liam lags behind, looking again at the house across the street, whose only light he can see is the blue smoldering of a TV in the front room. She watches TV in the dark while she waits for her husband to get home. Liam considers searching through the grass for his one-hit, but it's too risky. He steps toward the door in case Wendy is watching to see why he's not right behind her, but he can't break away from that house across the street yet, knows that sooner or later Wendy will have to quit her job, and he will have to take care of her and the kids between shifts at the deli, will probably never so enjoy those hours of slicing meat, because going home means being trapped inside his house at everyone's beck and call. Maybe he will have to quit too, and the furniture cheque will be the only thing coming in, with them hoping that his parents don't run the place into the ground before kicking off, sooner rather than later.

II - Pepper Steak

Inside, the house feels so much smaller than the garage. From the kitchen, while discreetly grasping the edge of the counter, Wendy hollers across the world, *"Ryan, why don't you do what your dad told you and get rid of that science project? Miranda, I want to see your homework."* The drill sergeant has arrived.

Ryan is still upstairs, and Miranda is in the other room with the computer, but the voice undoubtedly reaches him over the zombies coming out of the night to devour him, and undoubtedly penetrates her two-dimensional social existence, where comments popping up as type on the screen from who knows who are somehow more preferable and intimate than a voice on the telephone. Liam heard just last week that a boy hanged himself in his garage because somebody had been putting him down over the computer for months, which makes Liam wonder why, if the kid hated what they were saying so much, he just didn't turn off the goddamn computer and watch MTV for a while. The fact that Liam can't come up with a reason scares him suddenly. He doesn't know anything about his kids' world.

Why does Miranda attach herself to that screen every night? The question sinks into the murk of his high. He tries to hold onto those one-hits that soften his being inside this house with all them about to converge into the small space of the kitchen, but also make the whole scene slippery to him, like trying to hold onto the handle of the fork with buttery fingers.

Ryan hears it from her when he appears a few minutes later, a kid with a mushroom cap of brown hair, pale skin, and a sprinkling of freckles. He's changed out of his school shirt into an old camp T-shirt, and is already adopting the mopey look of the teenagers who come into the store on the weekend to buy frozen enchiladas and bottles of Mountain Dew to sustain them through weekend-long marathons of Grand Theft Auto or World of Warcraft, hypnotized blobs of brainless space. Ryan knows not to keep his mom waiting, although when she starts in on him, she's more focused on wiping away whatever somebody left in the sink. "Ryan, you've left that volcano here for a goddamn week and ignored your father telling you to put it somewhere. No Xbox through the weekend."

It's a threat she puts on Liam to uphold because most of that time she'll be at work, probably knows deep down he won't stick to his guns, but right now, the threat is all she's got.

Ryan's face drops as if he actually believes she'll enforce it, or maybe understands that if she finds out he knows the truth, she might feel compelled to show him that she means it this time. "No, Mom. Dad didn't tell me to put it away."

She glances at Liam, who is also hanging onto his edge of the counter, and it's in that moment that he feels the Xenon undercabinet lights baking his oily patch of largely exposed scalp, feels the immense weight of his black plastic frames dragging his head down in a slump and constantly sliding to the tip of his rosacea-blossomed nose, and feels the hug of his T-shirt around his belly, whose lingering moisture makes it as though he's come home wrapped up in Napoli salami.

Wendy is tearing some plastic off a piece of Styrofoam-packaged meat she's retrieved from the fridge. Liam knows he must've bought it from Marsh sometime, but he can't remember what it was or when that was, and he hopes she checked the 'use by' date before she threw away the cellophane. "Don't give me that. He told you sometime in the last week.

135

We both have, but you never listen." She and Liam both know Ryan is just five or so years shy of being completely outside their realm of control. At nine years old, his obedience already comes and goes.

It takes a second request for Miranda to appear. "I was in the middle of a conversation. Can I please go back and finish?"

"No, and typing isn't a conversation," Wendy says. "What about your homework?"

"We didn't have any." She opens a carton of day-old mini cinnamon rolls Liam brought home for tomorrow's breakfast, retrieves one and begins picking off each subsequent outside layer and popping it into her mouth. Miranda is supposed to wait until she's thirteen to receive a lesson in make-up application from her mother, but there is a definite shimmer to her lips that could be spit, or the remnants of lip gloss from her day at school. She has tried to sneak into her mom's three tubs of make-up on various occasions, but the girl is even more heavy-handed than her mother, doesn't understand the concept of less is more, and has never made it out the door before Wendy dragged her back to the bathroom to clean off the harlot mask. Maybe now she's finally become discreet enough to elude her mom's capture.

"Stop eating that. We're going to have…" One knee buckles again, and she has to mash herself into the oven door and latch onto the handle with both hands to keep herself from going down. The room remains in stasis until she flips the knob to preheat the oven, and puts the meat that Liam recognizes as pepper steak in a cooking pan. She would be better to do it on the stove, at least to sear it first, maybe apply some rub from the spice cabinet, but she contemplates the meat like something she doesn't know what do with beyond cooking it

136

to gray, and divvying slabs of shoe rubber to each of them. "How can you not have any homework out of four classes?"

"It's the weekend," she says. "Nobody gives homework on the weekend. Mr. Tellie says he's not going to do any planning or grading on the weekend, so why should he expect us to do any work?"

Wendy slides the pan into the oven, though it is far from preheated. "Mr. Tellie sounds pretty lazy to me, but that doesn't mean he can make you that way."

"Shows what you know. Mr. Tellie is my favorite teacher. Lots of kids' favorite." She pops the inner core of the cinnamon roll into her mouth.

"That doesn't mean he's a good teacher. He'd be my favorite too if he never gave homework on the weekends, but that doesn't mean I'd learn anything."

Miranda informs her mother that he is a good teacher, but then she is through with the conversation and goes into the living room to watch T.V.

Wendy opens the door to the stove as if to check the progress. "What am I supposed to do with this?" She closes the door again, but holds onto the handle and stares at the section of fleur-de-lis wallpaper that, after having been mottled with spattered bacon grease for fifteen years of Liam frying up a pound every Saturday, has turned to bubbles of mud. Nobody can say that he doesn't keep his family fed. He could do something with the pepper steak too, something to make them chew a little longer than necessary just to take in the taste, not gulp it down before they gag and wonder if they can face another bite. She says she wants him to take over, but she remains there hanging onto the oven door and fixated on the wallpaper, and he can't bring himself to try to pry her away. If she fails to move soon, the pores in the meat will be cooked closed, and it will be beyond his help.

He doesn't care as much about losing the meat as he does about losing a chance to glimpse the woman across the street. Another one might not come for days. Maybe she works some second shift job and is right then strolling out to her car. Maybe she dances for a living, maybe swivels around a pole at Déjà Vu, where Liam only ever went once ten years ago for Wendy's brother Ronnie's bachelor party the night before marrying that whackjob junkie, Tina something-or-other, who when she found out where he and his buddies had gone to celebrate, spent most of the reception berating Ronnie in front of everybody as a creep and pervert for going to one of those places to watch skanky women take their clothes off, and asking him what else he did with those skanks besides watch? Did he touch them? Was he sorry he didn't marry one of them instead of her? Were they prettier than her? Most all of them were, but Ronnie knew better than to say so.

That was the first day of a marriage that lasted a little over three years, during which whackjob junkie Tina something-or-other found occasion to take her clothes off for her boss, some guy she met at her NA meeting, the eighteen-year-old kid from down the street who cut their grass, and probably any number of guys who figured she wasn't so terrible-looking and why not, since she was so quick to offer? Since Ronnie went to a strip club the night before their wedding, guess that gave her the right.

Liam takes advantage of Wendy's moment of distraction to slip down the hallway to the windows next to the front door. Her voice reaches him just as he looks out across the street. *"Where'd you go? You told me you'd help me with dinner."* Her voice falls to mumbles, but he hears it. "Should've had it made already. You're the supposed chef. Why should I come home and have to mess with it?" Her car is still in the driveway across the street, and Jeff has since come home and parked behind her. The light shines through a couple of side windows that probably look into their kitchen. They must be making dinner together too. Maybe he's giving her grief for watching TV instead of cooking for him. Maybe he's some dumb bastard who doesn't have a clue what he has, will complain about her deficiencies until she up and leaves on him. Does she dance for him, or just when he's away, dancing only for Liam without even knowing, but she must know that if she dances with the shade halfway up, somebody might be watching. Does Kylie dance for her husband when he gets home after a week on the boat? Do they even talk to each other anymore, or do they chew their dinner in heavy silence? Does she pine for him when he's gone, or does she relish each time he leaves, dread every return, and hope this time the sea might take him from her forever?

Liam could probably find something out about Kylie on the computer, maybe send her a message from miles away that these days is more preferable and intimate than a phone call. He would need Miranda to help him with that, though, and with that help would come more questions than he wants to answer.

Wendy calls again. He tugs himself from the window, nothing to see anyway, but at least he's ruled out her working second shift. She's no public dancer.

Ryan clogs the hallway with the volcano propped in his arms; he speaks from behind it. "Can I just throw this out?"

Liam opens his mouth to protest. Over five hours they'd spent together, bending the wire into a cone, laying strips of plaster over it, painting it, and even fastening little plastic trees to the base. Liam kind of hoped that after the science fair, Ryan would hold onto it, maybe display it in his bedroom, so every once in a while, he could make it erupt for friends who came over. The thing is too enormous to fit on any surface in his room, though; Ryan can barely wrap his arms around it now, is about to drop it right here in the hall. The kid would have to shove it into his closet, another thing to take up space, another thing for him to toss his shoes on, or climb onto when he has to reach for something on the upper shelf, the plaster, paint, and work they shared mashed into crumbs to sprinkle away in the carpet and clog up Wendy's vacuum every Saturday. For the next couple of years, Liam will have to listen to her harangue Ryan about the mess she is dealing with until he finally hauls what's left of the thing to the curb like he should've done in the first place. The kid doesn't have any friends coming over to show it to these days anyway.

Liam squeezes past, and nods sure without looking at the volcano again. The kid probably needs help with the front door that Liam isn't going to give him. They worked too damn hard for a C+ and only one public eruption.

In the kitchen, Wendy has moved from the oven and is sitting at the kitchen table as if she's had enough. She pinches the corners of her eyes, squints, and then blinks a few times. The sink is clean, but she neglected to wipe the jelly ring off the countertop left from the making of Miranda's PBJ this morning.

Liam retrieves the pepper steak from the oven to find that she's tried to broil it, the outside already turned to concrete. He still sprinkles a sea salt steak rub over it, pats it in with his hands, and only thinks about washing them after he's done. Some taste at least. He never cooked before changing jobs from the hospital cafeteria to the deli. He's picked up a few recipes and cooking techniques since then. When you're surrounded by meat all day, what is there to talk about other than what to do with it? Bernie, who works behind the butcher counter adjacent to him, must cook every single meal on his charcoal grill, brags about using it to cook pizzas and Thanksgiving dinner. Liam used to char every burger he ever made on his grill, but now with Bernie's guidance, he's learned the secret of indirect heat and a perfect burger every time.

The pepper steak doesn't turn out half bad, the mouthfuls biting back. He accompanied it with corn out of a can and buttered slices of Wonder bread. Despite his effort, Wendy and the kids each work on their pieces of meat with the expressionless face of someone chewing on a piece of gum whose flavor has long gone to lead without a place available to spit it out. Wendy asks the kids how school was today, and both answer fine without slowing their jaws, probably keeping their mouths full to keep from having to elaborate. She doesn't ask how his day was in the deli. She knows his answer: same old, same old. She probably wouldn't take too kindly to him recounting the most interesting part of the day, when he trailed a woman, who looked so intriguing from the back, stealthily through the whole store to get a look at her face, just to see, only to find out it was nothing all that special, that she hadn't even bothered with make-up before leaving the house. That last part, Wendy might find interesting. She might ask him if he'd by chance gotten her number while stalking her, because if she doesn't know what to do with her face, Wendy can certainly help her in that department.

They finish off the evening all together, but separate, in front of the TV, watching a sitcom the two kids pick after both being vetoed from returning to the Xbox and computer in lieu of family time. The show is about two guys living with a girl, supposedly platonic roommates except the two guys both secretly are in competition for the girl. It reminds Liam of the old *Three's Company,* except not as funny, or maybe not funny at all. Maybe he just doesn't get it. He isn't sure why Miranda and Ryan picked it, because neither so much as smirks when the laugh tracks come coughing through the speakers to let them know that the last line was hilarious. Ryan sits cross-legged six inches from the television, maybe needing glasses like his mom but not owning up to it, and Miranda, in her my-parents-are-such-an-embarrassment phase, wears a gripe on her face and is crammed against the arm of the couch with her head lopsidedly propped up on her forearm, sitting as far as possible from her mother on the other end. Wendy is already nodding off, her head falling back every few seconds, meeting the cushion, and then vaulting forward again to vertical before anyone notices.

By the time the show is over, Wendy has given in, her head lopped back on the cushion, her hair walling in her ears, and her red, smeared lips, chunky from the salt-rubbed dinner, gaping open and slogging up air. Miranda asks Liam if she can quickly check something on the computer, which will take her just as long as it takes Liam or Wendy to discover her still clinging to the screen and tell her to get off. Liam nods, which opens the door for Ryan to ask if he can resume the game that he's been playing for weeks and has no conceivable end. Liam feels sucked in, but he nods again. What else can he do?

He is left to sink further into his floral chair, worn to thread in the center where he's spent entirely too much time of his life. Wendy redecorates like she cleans, haphazardly fixing one spot and leaving the rest in shambles. Just last weekend, she bought a new lamp to go on the side table almost too rickety to hold it. Another weekend, she brought home a Ficus plant for the front hall when all the other plants around this place are shriveled husks that she's forgotten to take care of. Then last summer, she bought a new coffee table, though the old one held his beer can just fine, and yet this chair remains, leaving Liam to worry his ass is going to drop right through to the floor every time he sits down in it.

With his wife conked out on the nearby couch at 8:30, he retrieves an Olympia from the fridge, one of two he has left. He should've thought of it being Friday night and brought a twelve-pack home with him from work. In his pocket is a balled up bag of weed, maybe a half dozen more hits, but by now his one-hit is lost, probably permanently clogged with mud and rotted leaves, to be discovered by the neighborhood kids running through the yard who used to ring the doorbell to see if Ryan could come out to play, but don't come around anymore. Ryan doesn't seem to miss them as long as he has a control pad in hand. Those kids are probably right now taking turns letting Liam's one-hit hang out of their mouths like James Dean or some other rebel they're never going to be. Maybe Liam will go on out and try to find it after this beer is finished, when his kids are too absorbed in their digital worlds and Wendy too deep in sleep for anybody to notice him slip out.

The show has changed to a kid at a spelling bee, his mom grilling him backstage, word after word—*vacuous, amendment, plethora*—and he repeats them, letter by letter, sounding like a Dictaphone. A freckle-cheeked girl behind him, whom his mother can't see, wrinkles her face and sticks a mean tongue out at him, and for a moment, he smiles, causing his mother to jostle him to pay attention. Given the chance, that type of girl would only be nasty to him, but once she leaves, he remains fixated on where she stood, unwilling to utter even one more letter to his mother from then on. Maybe it's supposed to be funny, but with no laugh track, Liam doesn't know what to do with this show. He drinks the beer that tastes so close to water. Tomorrow he really needs to splurge on something with a little bite. He doesn't want to start drinking his beer like they eat their pepper steak, going through the motions just to get it down.

III - Through the Glass

He leaves the TV going because Wendy will invariably wake up without voices around her, would never tolerate the world abandoning her. He makes his way down the hallway and out the front door. Night has come down fully now, with the chisel of lingering winter in the breeze, and though he could've used the front light to help locate his one-hit, he resists turning it on and advertising his position on the lawn.

Across the street, the kitchen light is still lit, but all he can see are the windows shining onto the walk-up side porch. He makes his way along the front of his house, freezing near a bush as a car comes around the corner out of nowhere and blasts him with light. When it's gone, he sweeps a boot through the grass to try and hear the tink of the metal one-hit against his sole. Nothing but brittle, crushed dead lawn. No more getting high tonight unless he fashions something together from inside, maybe a wooden spool to suck it through, or a copper piece of plumbing with a little metal screen on the end. He made a volcano out of chicken wire, so anything is possible.

He moves further, sticking close to the house beyond the reach of the streetlamp that shines at the edge of their lot. When he travels far enough to get an angle on the dual kitchen windows tucked at the back of the porch, he is left looking at two curtain sheers turned opaque from this distance. A wisp of shadow crosses over them and vanishes. The kitchen is supposed to be the most occupied room in the house, but Liam stays in his—with its gold appliances, bubbling Formica countertops, and linoleum so ground with dirt you could plant seeds in it—only long enough to put something together for a meal or get a beer out of the fridge. What's so great about the kitchen across the street that they're spending the whole night in it? He's almost as eager to get a look at the room as he is her. Debbie. The name suddenly comes to him from the short conversation he had with the guy as they both stared down at the fallen S mailbox in his yard. 'Debbie and I looked at so many houses before we found this one,' Jeff had said. They were transferred from Memphis because of his job, and it worked out because Debbie, with her field, could get a job about anywhere.

Liam no longer remembers what her field is, but he can rule out pole dancer because he's pretty sure he'd remember hearing that. Maybe she's a nurse who makes all the male patients drool over themselves, or maybe an elementary school teacher who all the boys have a crush on and attach mirrors to the toes of their shoes to see what she's hiding under that skirt of hers.

Liam crouches as he moves along the property line between his and the Schleaners' property, standing up when he considers that either Dan or Betty or any of their four kids might be watching through the window right then, and wondering why he is moving through their yard like a commando.

When he hits the street, he glances for traffic before darting in an arc beyond the street light's reach, feeling his belly chug up and down over his belt and his breath quicken after the short burst. He needs to start taking walks around the neighborhood in the evenings to get some exercise like he planned to do all last summer, but only made it out a few times before giving it up. Maybe when it gets warmer. He pushes the glasses up his already sweaty nose, and takes a swig of his beer which has been jostled to foam. He ends up in the expansive property of the guy on the corner who owns twice as much lawn as Liam, but with twice as much to mow. Liam could easily use a push mower to do his lot, probably good exercise, but the riding mower his father gave to him after buying a new one completes the job in about 20 minutes instead of an hour.

He moves toward their driveway with a dark blue Silverado in front and a black Infinity Sedan in the back. Somebody is taking advantage of making more money. He creeps along the back bumper of the Infinity so he can casually move to the street like a passerby in case they catch sight of him. Through the panels in the window he can begin to see the pink of their faces; they are sitting down.

He sidles alongside the cars up the driveway, too close to make a break for it without being seen. The porch runs along the side and around the front of the house with no railing, just a few posts to hold the roof over it. It's far too exposed for anybody to ever sit out on, least of all the Sullys, the prior residents who owned the property for at least as many years as Liam has owned his, and who, after they retired, never left the house if at all possible. At the back end of the porch, atop the steps next to the windows, is the door Jeff and Debbie must use as the main entrance into the kitchen, despite there being another door in the front. Visitors must be confused as to which to knock on.

The picture in the windows delineates them slightly as he gets closer. They are sitting at a table about a foot from each other, and he recognizes Jeff by his closely-cropped hair, and Debbie by the unrolled ball that now hangs down her neck. Her face looks like a mess of pixels, like the bleary characters who wander the world of his son's game Minecraft. Worse graphics than the Atari Pitfall game back in the 80's, which provided Liam no more than a half hour of entertainment

147

before he abandoned his controller to go play outside, yet Ryan can spend hours upon hours looking at blocks on the screen. Maybe the world has just gotten that boring for kids.

Liam mounts the steps, clutching the railing to keep his weight off the potentially whiny stairs. In the shadows beyond the streetlamp, he should be as invisible as the darkness. He steps onto the porch, is only three feet away from the windows. She appears to be laughing, her legs crossed and the top one bouncing in rhythm with her outbursts. She might be attractive, but the curtains still obscure her, a wedding veil over her face that everyone waits to have lifted to see how she looks on the prettiest day of her life. It's all downhill—marriage, kids, working, bickering, blame, resentment, indifference—from there.

Liam might've turned around there, but it's not good enough, like it's not good enough to see only the gym-toned arms or the tight can or the back of her head as she passes by the deli counter. It all comes back to the face, like searching for someone from whom he's become separated at a massive concert, chasing every familiar hairstyle up ahead, wedging between sluggish and malicious bodies to close the distance, losing sight of her before finding her then losing her again, finally reaching out between two immovable strangers to grab for her shoulder, and turning her around only to find he's gotten the wrong person again, always that terrifying thought as he scans the crowd of unfamiliar faces that maybe she isn't even out there to be found.

He moves closer, and a board chirps and seizes him up. The weather's still too cold to have the windows open, and they just keep on talking, her bouncing leg sometimes kicking his knee. They're drinking something green in cocktail glasses. He continues, pushing his glasses up again and venturing to

148

within a foot of the window, his form as invisible as the darkness. Another six inches and the veil over her face turns transparent, revealing the bulges in her hair where, after dancing, she tucked away the dislodged strands, tying it into less a ponytail than a pig's tail. Her glass hovers near a mouth so happy, alternately drinking, talking, and laughing with white teeth biting the air. Her gorgeous, hooked nose could've busted clean through this window and tapped him on the cheek without any other part of her face even meeting the glass, that nose such an obstacle for anybody who kissed her, not Jeff with the button stuck to his face, but certainly Liam who has a trunk of his own. The two of them would've required air traffic controllers to time their approaches, needed to spar for position, made contact like a hammer lock, and with his glasses to maneuver around, forget about it. While he contemplates its plausibility, he forgets about his proximity. That's when his glasses shoot forward down his nose and rap against the window.

He marvels as she finally looks at him straight on, shows him everything, like turning to face him in a crowd. That is enough for him. He could've slipped down the steps across the street and returned to his show about the spelling bee without thinking about her ever again. The conversation on the other side of the window ceases, and they both lock on him. Had he been in the aisle of the grocery store, he would've reached past her and straightened whatever crooked box or can happened to be at his disposal. Out here he's blowing in the wind. Wrong house maybe. Wrong house. He had too many Olympias down at Mumford's Tavern and damned if he didn't walk up to the wrong house. He gives them an idiotic half-wave he hopes they translate as sorry and turns back toward his house.

149

No more than two steps later, though, hands latch onto the back of his shirt, and his beer clonks onto the porch and rolls off into the grass. Jeff swivels him around and grabs at the slack in Liam's shirt, asks him, "What the fuck do think you're doing looking in our window?"

IV - Block Party

J eff's question is at least 80 proof. Liam tries to formulate his excuse. Wrong house is all. Just a mistake. Before he can, Jeff lets go of him.

"Hey...you, from across the street."

"Liam."

"Yeah, Liam. Hey, sorry about that. I thought you were some kind of..." He stalls on what he thought. "Come on in and sit down."

Liam is left holding his excuse while Jeff puts an arm around him, ushering him through the side door inside, the arm hanging off him like a yolk, Liam's steps about to punch right through the floor. He's led through a dimly lit mudroom stacked with the paint cans, balled-up drop cloths, and the scattered tools of weekend renovations, into the kitchen within the pane of glass and the wedding veil. Jeff seems overjoyed to introduce him. "Honey, this is..."

"Liam."

"Liam. He lives right across the street. He's our neighbor. This is Debbie, the love of my life."

"Our neighbor, huh," she says. He can't see her through the glass suctioned to her face. She drains her drink to the shallows of her ice cubes, losing one out the side. After she removes the glass, a wet line remains on her face where the cube made its escape route.

"Debbie just made up a pitcher of margaritas." He takes a drink and roils from the taste. "Tart sons of bitches. Get Liam here one, will you?" He still has a hand on Liam's shoulder, fingers turned into pinchers.

Debbie floats from the table and drifts to the counter, where the pitcher sits with two inches left in the bottom. "We're about out." She grasps hold of the handle, and lifts her own glass near the spout.

"Don't worry about it," Liam says. She has her back to them, and he waits for her to turn around again. He doesn't think he's yet gotten a full-on look at her without a curtain filtering his vision.

"Make up another batch. It's Friday night. You can't go home this early. Sit down." Jeff leads him to the table, and Liam takes a seat in one of the high-backed dark wooden throne chairs that seem to encase him, and have the hard feel underneath him, like he is sitting on a pew at St. Joseph's, the Catholic church that he and Wendy used to take the kids to every week, but over the past few years have fallen out of practice, only making it back on Christmas and Easter, and sometimes not even then. He is forced to sit at exactly 90 degrees vertical. No dozing off in one of these, and he wonders why, with all the places to lounge in a house after a long week of work, they chose here.

With her back to them, Debbie takes the bottle of Patron and the two-liter bottle of kiwi-colored mix from the fridge, which she shakes in the air. "We're okay on tequila. It's the mix we're running low on. After this one, it's going to have to be shots." She concocts another batch behind the cover of her tie-dye shirt. She wears stretch pants, which must make it easy to bend her body any way the music takes her. As Jeff finishes off his own drink, Liam slides a look at her can, thinks it looks decent, but doesn't take too long on it. It's all about the face, grasping for that shoulder in the crowd and turning her around to see who's there.

152

The kitchen is silent, while Jeff finishes off the dregs of his drink, probing with his tongue for an ice cube to suck on while he waits for a refill.

"What were you doing out there, Liam?" Debbie asks.

Out on the porch with the darkened street around them, the wrong house didn't seem so unbelievable, but in here it seems ludicrous, especially since he's neglected to portray himself as too sloshed to make it home. "I just saw the light on—"

Jeff grinds the ice cube between his molars. "What do you do, Liam?" He's on a different station.

Liam tells him.

"I've never been to that store. We shop at Kroger. But I drive past it every day on my way to work." He might've been telling somebody that he's never been to Europe, but he's always wanted to go, will make it there someday.

"I'm up to 35 hours. I'd like to get it up to 40, but I have to wait on some turnover. The shifts are all over the place, but if I need a day off, they're good about it. Last weekend, I wanted to take the kids to the Deerfield Fair on Saturday. No problem. They gave me it off."

Jeff is beholding the copper rooster mold above the stove as if wondering how long that's been hanging there. Debbie returns with two jigger glasses and the pitcher. She fills them, and apologizes for no lime as she slides one over to Liam; Jeff forgot them at the store. It's not until he lifts it to take a drink that Liam realizes she gave him hers, a smudged pink crescent along the rim where she's kissed the glass. She has claimed the other glass without noticing, and he can't help rotating his before drinking to line the impression up with where his mouth will land.

153

She stares past Jeff at Liam over the top of her tilted glass, holds on him until she gulps three times and sets down her glass, her eyes tight but so plain compared to Wendy's outlined, shadowed, and mascaraed set that always seem to be looking out at him from inside a deep cave. "Saw the light on? We've lived here for three weeks, and we've had the lights on every night. Why didn't you come over before now? And do you go next door and look in their windows when you see their lights on?"

Jeff is too busy christening his drink to break in with his easy conversation. "I just realized," Liam says. "That I haven't been around to say hello. You being new to the neighborhood."

"No cake?" she says. Liam doesn't understand the question. That nose—too bad he couldn't see it from the side again to really appreciate it. "No bottle of Scotch? No birdhouse?...Usually when you want to welcome somebody to the neighborhood, aren't you supposed to bring something?"

The last thing she needs is another birdhouse. Maybe he should've stuck to the wrong house excuse. He retreats to his drink now, the tartness pinching at the underside of his tongue, the octane coming afterward and strafing his sinuses. Debbie doesn't make them tame. "I just wanted to say hello. I'm sure my wife will bake you something tomorrow. She's been meaning to." The truth is, Wendy hasn't even mentioned their new neighbors, might not even know the house was sold. And she hasn't baked anything for as long as he can remember.

She twirls her finger in the already exposed ice cubes, turning her drink into the spin cycle. "Well, don't show up empty-handed again."

"We got to have you guys over this weekend," Jeff says. "A barbecue tomorrow. How about that? How many of you are there?"

"Four. We got two kids."

"A boy and a girl right? I've seen them heading off to school."

"Do you have kids?" The house must have at least three bedrooms. What else would they fill them with except kids, and what else besides kids is left for a young couple to do with their lives after they get married, nail down careers, and buy a house?

"No." Jeff says. A drink and no more information or questions to follow.

"Sounds great," Liam says. He wants to reverse the conversation. "About the barbecue. I can get a discount on the meat. 25% off if you get it at Marsh. Just tell me what you need."

Jeff nods. "We can do that." He's drawn to the rooster again, and his response is something floating in another room, how his speech would've sounded before, when Liam was still out on the porch, not a member of the room, had Liam put his ear, not his head, against the glass.

"Just wanted to say hello at nine o'clock at night?" Debbie says. Her top lip sits on the rim of the glass, but she doesn't drink. That lip is pomegranate, though it appears most of her lipstick was left behind on the rim of his glass. Some people don't need to cover it all up.

He nods, surveys the walls, painted sunshine yellow with a tile backsplash that wasn't there the only time he ever had the occasion to be in the Sullys' kitchen over the years of living across the street from them. That was two days after Harry Sully collapsed onto the hull of the rowboat he was

155

refurbishing in the driveway, a massive cardiac arrest. The event brought an ambulance, a fire engine, and two cop cars, their lights all cutting through Liam's living room as they tried to revive him. Following the funeral two days later, Joan invited all the attendees back to the house for a spread of bagels that crunched like peanut brittle, and Dunkin Donuts' boxed coffee as tepid as day-old dishwater, both tasting like they'd been bought as soon as he flatlined and been sitting out on the table the two days since then, awaiting the arrival of so many people looking for free food.

"You've done a lot of work in here," he says. "I saw the kitchen before, but only once." The cabinets look new too, blonde with no knobs. Maybe they haven't gotten around to drilling them yet. The kitchen seems much brighter and more open now, even in the night, than it had been on the day he saw it, so crowded with shadows and gloom, shades drawn half-mast, and the room crammed with people clad in black and grays, all choking down hunks of bagel that clawed the backs of their throats, squeezing out small talk about the wonderful spread of food, the amazing work done on the house, or the touching service, anything, it seemed, to avoid talking about Harry when he was alive. Most of the attendees seemed to know him no better than Liam, who had only shared maybe a half-dozen sidewalk conversations with the guy in all the time they lived across the street from each other, always about some wood project he was working on in his garage, the S mailbox, or the birdhouse, or the Adirondack chair for his back porch, and always with a step-by-step explanation of how he was going about it, as if Liam was taking notes and afterward would run home and start constructing his own.

"Try not gawking inside people's windows," Debbie says. "Probably be invited inside more often."

156

"They were older, the people who used to live here. Kept to themselves." Joan had always done her best to avoid eye contact with Liam if he happened to be outside when she was leaving or coming home, precluding her from having to wave or ask how the flowers were coming in, but when she came home to find her husband that day, she came howling out into middle of the street for somebody to help him, somebody to call somebody, somebody who knew CPR. Liam quit getting dressed for work and called the ambulance, then went over with a half dozen neighbors to where Joan was hollering in the driveway. Harry was sitting in a folding chair in the garage, his head resting on the bottom of his upturned boat propped up on saw horses, the putty knife having fallen to the floor at his feet. He had already gone gray.

Jeff sprawls back in his chair, splaying his legs and arms like somebody giving up. "It never ends. I'm at it all weekend, but tonight, I told her I'm taking the night off."

"Don't you mean Home Depot is at it all weekend? They put in this new kitchen."

"I painted it."

"That's the worst part," she says, scanning the line where wall meets ceiling to note the jaggedness of his strokes. Liam must've misread the mood in here. Maybe they were just laughing at each other before, drinking to endure the other's mockery. Maybe it would warm up between them if Jeff knew about her dancing.

Jeff asks her for a refill, and she fills them all, the last of the pitcher sliding over the side of Liam's glass. Halfway through this round, the mood seems to soften. "What's the deal with this neighborhood?" she says. "Nobody else has been around to welcome us, and nobody'll even wave when they drive past the house."

157

"Most of them keep to themselves," Liam says. "Unless you run your mower too early, or park your car in front of their house."

"Well, I'll tell you what," Jeff says. He's propping his head on his hand and leaning so far into it that his cheek is shoving up into his eye and squishing it. "Tomorrow, I'm going to go up and down this block and invite every last one of them to the barbecue. We'll make it a block party like we used to have when we were kids. You ever have one of those?" Liam nods. The whole block spilled out of their houses into the street. Liam's dad grilled hot dogs and kielbasa right in front of their driveway, Mr. Hall cooked burgers in front of his, and Mr. Cummins passed out cans of Budweisers to anybody over eighteen, and some who weren't. Kids ran around the middle of the street tossing Frisbees and Nerf footballs without having to worry about getting run over, hanging out in anybody's garage or on anybody's lawn they pleased, because the owner was undoubtedly stumbling somewhere on the street, unaware of their flowers being trampled or screen door being run through. Everybody letting loose. Liam isn't sure he's ever known true freedom in his life, but that day was damn close.

"I'll call the cops and get a permit to block off the street," Jeff goes on. "Maybe get a couple kegs and hire a band. It'll be epic."

"Big plans," Debbie says. She's looking down and tracing her finger along a fissure in the tabletop. She's heard them before.

"Hey," Liam says. Their glasses are drained, but he wants to keep things rolling in the right direction. "Do you guys get high? Because—" He pulls out the rest of his quarter that's been reduced to an amount no bigger than a thimble, the

158

baggie crunched so much in his pocket that the plastic has turned to milk.

"What is that?" Debbie says.

Jeff reaches out and pinches the bag. "It's all seeds, man. Let me show you." He leaves the table, and returns with a wooden cigar box, rotates it toward Liam, and opens it to display its contents like it's a ring box and he's about to propose. Inside are his-and-her pipes, a couple of lighters, and a bag rolled over itself and stuffed to the size of a cucumber. "You got to buy in bulk and from a reputable source, or all you get out of it is cancer."

He proceeds to pack one of the pipes, and passes it to his wife. With the funnel-shaped metal protruding from her mouth, she flicks the lighter over and over to produce only sparks, finally getting it lit, and watching cross-eyed to make sure the flame gets sucked inside. With the pipe bobbing in her mouth, she's diminished somehow. Maybe she's the girl back in high school who, after doing everything right for so long, is willing to break all of her parents' crushing rules to escape into the edgy crowd, wants to seem cool enough for once in her life. She just isn't there yet, can't quite pull it off, but give her some time, and she will. Liam likes how that nose pinches as she inhales, though.

One turn with that pipe would've been plenty for him, what with the tequila roaring like a river through his skull. The first hit is like the colossal collision of a baseball bat to his forehead, but he accepts two or three more pass-arounds, can't really remember the number, and vacuums in as much each time as his lungs will bear, before hacking up each one like a fool.

The laughter is constant now. Jeff keeps carving out his plan for the block party, and now Debbie seems to buy into

159

the idea, saying she'll make a jug of her margaritas and fix up a bucket of her famous homemade guacamole. "We'll shake up this neighborhood and see what falls out."

"Good luck," Liam says.

She raises a hand above her head and points at the ceiling like a spear. "The moles are finally going to come out of their holes and see what daylight looks like." With his cheek planted onto the tabletop, Jeff raises his empty glass in solidarity.

Liam thinks how he and Wendy don't know anybody around here after so many people moving out and moving in, Miranda neither, and Ryan's few neighborhood pals have abandoned him. Liam's parents knew about everybody on their block, and he knew every kid up to three years older and younger, always had somebody to hang out with and never stayed inside unless he was grounded or the sky was falling in on them. Why can't they have that here? Why can't it start right in this kitchen? The moles out of their holes. That's right. Tomorrow.

Eventually Liam drags himself from the table and mumbles that he really needs to get home. Jeff manages a wave while snoozing on the table, but Debbie follows Liam to the door. She holds the door to the mud room open, and walks through it with him to the outside porch. She braces herself in the door frame, her knees wobbling back and forth in a jittery movement he tries to connect with what he saw of her upstairs. This isn't music, but maybe a chill or whatever was in that pipe that she wasn't ready for. "So glad to know we have a fun neighbor. We were starting to think we were going to be outcasts. Wouldn't be the first time."

She really is like Kylie, a girl who just wanted to rattle the world, except Liam didn't have enough internal combustion to help her do the job. He knows now, looking at Debbie, that the person he was looking for in all those women he chased through the grocery store was Kylie. Had to be. He'd had so little with her—just the taste of her tongue and the frustrating touch of her harnessed breasts—but in that little bit, she was perfect, perfect if only in her potential. "It was good to meet you," he says, and because he can think of nothing else to say, "you're a really good dancer."

Her head rests against the frame as if she's about to go to sleep, her features without corners, but then she's upright, tensile bands surfacing in her neck. She waits for him to explain.

"I saw you up in your window today. Earlier. Dancing around."

"You saw me? I was just…How long were you watching?" Her hand slides down the door frame and falls off to her side.

Being so stoned makes the truth seem benign. "Twenty minutes maybe."

"You were watching for 20 minutes? You stood in your front yard and watched me for 20 minutes?"

"No, I was in my garage for most of the time." He takes a step back, is suddenly a lot more sober than he was fifteen seconds ago, and feels the same need to make a break for it as when he was caught looking in their window.

She looks a lot more sober too. "Where do you get off looking in people's windows?"

He's pretty sure now that Jeff doesn't know about her dancing. Maybe nobody knows. "I just happened to see you…"

"You just happened to see me and watch me from inside your garage. What were you doing in there all that time while you were watching me?"

"Just watching. Just watching, and smoking a little. That's all."

She steps out onto the porch, but maintains an outstretched hand against the wall. "So it happened to be today that you decided to be neighborly?" Her words sound like a rake through gravel. "Just come over to meet the new couple." Her wobbly knee juts to the side, but she recovers, her voice holding steady. "You weren't coming over here to say welcome."

She advances, is at least three inches taller than he is. He backs up toward the front of the house, isn't sure how close the edge of the porch is. He might topple with his next step, but he can't look back. He glances in his periphery down the block. In the five houses he sees, there are maybe three lights on in total. What time is it? 9:30…10:00? On a Friday night. What made him think they could shake up this neighborhood?

"You were just trying to get another look. You *were* peeping in our window, and we caught you. You weren't going to knock at all." The light from the window drapes her with shadows, dark hammocks under her eyes, and from her nose, a pocket of darkness cleaved into one cheek.

"I liked how you danced. That's why I watched so long. Watching how you moved, it was like I could hear the music from across the street." This is probably the most interesting thing he's said all night. She stops, but he doesn't. "But I couldn't see your face, so when I saw your light on, I just wanted to see what you looked like."

"You like how I dance?" A turn of her face, and the shadows are flushed away as the inside light slaps over her. She

162

looks through the glass, maybe at Jeff passed out at the table, or maybe just away from Liam. "I don't know what I was even doing up there. Being stupid. I should've closed the blinds. The whole street is probably laughing about it right now."

"No, you were great. I would've watched longer, but..." He resists mentioning Wendy coming home. "Does he like your dancing?" It's a miracle he finds the name. "Jeff?"

"We only dance at weddings." She focuses on one of the cars in the driveway, turns and leans her back against the house. "And that's only if I drag him out on the floor. Math people. If he doesn't have a calculator in front of him, he's lost in the world. He's petrified to let people see him move. He latches onto me the whole time and won't let go. We end up stomping in circles to some industrial beat like it's 'Open Arms'."

Liam isn't too different. They only dance at weddings too. At Wendy's brother Ronnie's wedding, Wendy rotated her chair toward the dance floor as soon as the DJ started spinning, studied the dancers through the first three numbers, padding her feet in front of her chair and pistoning her shoulders. Then she turned to ask him to dance. He managed to put her off until he'd finished off at least six Heinies from the open bar, about the regular dosage of courage he needs to get him out there to move like a pendulum, crush some toes, and clap his hands like a two-year-old trying to keep rhythm with 'The Hokey Pokey'. At least he can stand on his own when he finally goes out there. "Well, he doesn't know what he's missing." He reaches to push his glasses back, but stops himself. Let 'em sag.

"That's nice to say." She pushes herself from the side of the house, but her step catches on one of the boards and vaults forward. He reaches an arm out to keep her from plunging over the edge, and she hooks her arm around his

163

neck, nearly taking them both over. Had he not been standing beside the pole, she would've. She lets out a burst of laughter before hauling herself to her feet, not removing her arm from around the back of his neck. Her laughter vanishes, and she looks at him, her face muddled over the tops of his glasses that he wishes now he had shoved back on his head so he could see her up close.

His belly takes up too much of the space between them, and he sucks it back millimeter by millimeter. Hopefully, she doesn't realize he's holding it in for her.

"Sometimes," she says, syllables like a breeze shushing through a screen. "You need to hear that you're good at something…that you're nice to look at. You don't always get that from who you're married to."

Liam sure doesn't get it from Wendy, but then again, she doesn't get it from him. Didn't she like his pepper steak? He'd turned it into something edible. How about the soft light he put in the bathroom to replace the fluorescent tubing, so she could get ready in the morning looking like a human being in the glass instead of a cadaver on the autopsy table. Maybe he'll start noticing when she comes back from the salon, tell her that he likes the new color, or comment that he likes the basket of dried flowers she put on the table in the hallway, and how she has such a good eye for brightening things up around their house.

Liam has sucked his stomach in so far that his rib cage actually sticks out further over the top of it, has to stifle his breath to keep it in. When her body caves against his, he forgets anything else he could've told Wendy that she might be needing to hear.

"I won't forget you said it." She kisses him on the cheek, holds it there just an instant so he won't forget, and separates herself from him. She takes a step back to shed his arm from around her. "Well, I need to go in and start making my guacamole. It's better if it sits overnight." She shambles away from him along the porch and into the house, with Liam watching her until the door closes behind her, waiting there another fifteen seconds to make sure it doesn't open again. The only thing she's in any condition to do tonight is go to bed. The only question is whether she'll leave Jeff resting on the table or haul him upstairs with her. Liam feels such a need to know that he's tempted to reclaim his place at the window to find out.

Instead he strolls back toward his house, taking his time with each step, enjoying the buzz that, with the tension gone, has settled back over him as if he's submerged himself into a steaming hot bath. The chill of the night is only on his temples and in his lungs as he breathes in each time, making every other part of him that much warmer.

What can he make for tomorrow? Short ribs maybe. Bernie must have a killer recipe to melt the meat off the bones. Maybe some homemade potato salad on the side, not the crap the little old lady makes in the back of Marsh every few days and stuffs into plastic tubs. Or maybe he should do pulled-pork burritos, something to go with her margaritas and guacamole. They can make the whole thing Mexican, tell everyone to wear something bright and bring something south-of-the-border style.

As he reaches his door, he turns back and as he suspected, the light is on in their bedroom behind the fully closed shade, the speed of it making him think that Jeff is going to spend the night in the kitchen while she has the bed to herself. He waits a moment to see her shadow sweep across the blind, even the tiniest infraction in the light, but it remains

165

constant. He imagines her sprawled out on the bed, unable to pull the sheets down as the room hums like a swarm of wasps around her, and she tries to determine if she's yet crossed over from feeling good to feeling ill. Maybe she's clinging to what Liam said and how good it made her feel. He just knows that when the next woman goes strolling past the deli counter, he won't go chasing her. His tailing days are over. She isn't Kylie, but none of them are, and none of them ever will be. This is just about as close as he's going to get.

The light behind the blind stays constant. He gives up and goes inside, expecting the house to be exactly as he left it, Ryan on his game in his room, Miranda on the computer in hers, and Wendy obliviously sucking up the night, nobody even knowing he was gone at all. Instead, what meets him inside the door is pandemonium.

V - Taking the Wheel

The screaming he hears freezes him in the darkened front hall, as he tries to figure out if it's coming from the television. It doesn't. First he hears Wendy's voice, filling up the house, *"You got to send somebody right away. There's blood everywhere."*

Liam notices a nickel-sized drop of it on the stairs, the color in the darkness turned the color of the dirty motor oil he drains out the bottom of the car every couple of months. More drops are present on the landing and going in a disjointed line toward the living room where Wendy's voice is erupting.

She seems to be talking on the phone, because she lags for a response. Miranda's frantic sobs come from another room. *"No Mom, tell them no. I don't want them to send anyone. Everyone will know. They'll all know—"* Her words crash into gasps.

Wendy addresses her, calling across the room. *"Keep hold of that, Honey, or you're going to bleed to death."* Miranda tells her no, tells her it was a mistake, just a mistake.

"That is no mistake."

Liam can't move from where his back is plastered against the front door, hopes it will all just blow over before he reemerges. Next to his feet is the volcano, the center hole bottomless beneath the shadows. With nobody to help him with the front door, Ryan has abandoned it just inside, where it might remain for another month until somebody cares enough to drag it down to the curb. It might just as easily remain there forever.

"She looks gray," Wendy says. "She looks gray." Her voice is slow and slurry, like she'd just been drinking margaritas

167

across the street. "Okay, bring her in? I'll bring her right in...No I'm okay to drive. We'll be there."

Liam finally ventures forward, following the oil spots, toward the kitchen. He hears the clip of her phone being shut.

"I'm not going there. It'll stop. I'll just wrap it up. I don't know why I did it."

"I don't know why either." Wendy's shoes thud across the linoleum, the erratic clumsy steps of somebody trying to walk a heavy bureau across the floor by tilting it this way and that. Liam catches a glimpse of her as she shuffles to the living room. "God I'm stepping in it. It's everywhere." Liam is aware that he isn't watching where he is stepping either, and he must be tracking it everywhere. Wendy goes on. "You need stitches. They have to check you out. "

"It was no big deal. I just had the knife and I ran it over my skin, and then it felt good, so I did it again. I didn't know it was cutting me." Her voice melts again, and she keeps repeating that she's not going, sounding like somebody who can't swim and spills out a gasp for help each time she clears the surface.

"How could you forget a knife can cut you? Where is your father? Where did he go? How could neither of you see him leave? How come he's always disappearing when something important is going on?"

Liam hurries toward the voices now. Here he is. Wendy is standing in the middle of the living room, her legs splayed out unnaturally to better support her failing balance. In front of her sits Miranda, stooped forward on the couch with one hand clamping one of their washcloths to her wrist, a splotch of red seeping outward into the beige cotton beyond her fingers. Her face is concrete. Wendy is right. She does look gray. She is shaking her head that she's not going.

Ryan sits in the chair usually occupied by Liam during the long evenings, and the boy notices his dad first. Though Ryan hasn't said anything since Liam came in and isn't crying or hollering—he's just sitting there, but it's the way he sits, on the very edge of the chair, gawking at his sister when most of the time he pretends she doesn't even exist, staring now as if he's trying to figure out who she is, or what she is. Seeing him there scares Liam the most.

Wendy picks up on Ryan's shift in focus and turns on Liam, her hair a matted mess that will be hell to brush through tomorrow morning. *"Where the hell have you been? You're supposed to be here. I've been looking all over for you. Your car was in the driveway. Where were you?"* She teeters on her legs, her calves looking no wider than broomsticks coming out of her skirt. She needs to switch to pants soon. There is less and less of her every day.

He tries to think of an excuse, but he didn't think he'd need one, can't find one now. Usually, she will hit him with a fusillade of questions, pick apart his story, not to find the truth in it so much as the lie. This time she doesn't bother. It doesn't matter.

"Do you realize what's going on here? Do you have any idea what went on here?"

He shakes his head, the buzz lifting slowly like when he forgets to open the fireplace flue, and after the living room fills with smoke, they have to open the windows, choke it out of their lungs, and wait for it to ooze outside, replaced by more cold than they started with.

"Ryan went into Miranda's room, and she was cutting her wrists." Tears melt her eyeliner and bleed out black over her cheeks.

"I wasn't cutting my wrists," Miranda says. "I just liked how it felt, the knife. It felt good."

169

"You were cutting your wrists. You did, for God sakes, and if Ryan didn't come in when he did, you would've cut the other one. You would've bled to death." His wife goes on. "Over some bastard. He said something to her...on the computer. She wasn't supposed to be on that anymore tonight." She jabs a look at Liam and then turns back to her daughter and places a palm on her back to initiate her moving. "Get in the car. We have to hurry. What did he say, Honey?"

Liam feels like he's receded from the room again, is standing in another part of the house listening to their conversation from behind a corner, with nobody even realizing he is there.

Miranda complies with standing up, maintaining hold of her wrist. "Nothing. He's not a bastard. He was just trying to be funny."

"Why would you defend him? What did he say that would make you do that?"

"Nothing, Mom. I'm not defending him. It was a joke." Her face is craggy and dark from crying, like a cherry shrinking in the sun just before it falls off the tree. She gazes downward as if she needs to watch her feet fall onto the carpeting, "It just wasn't funny. He meant it to be, but it wasn't."

She's locked arm-in-arm with her mother and lunges forward in her steps, hauling both of them forward. Liam reaches out to stop them from falling over, but they catch their footing without needing him.

Wendy leads her toward the hall, and Ryan trails behind. All Liam can think to do is step out of the way. They move past without so much as a look. He goes last, and as he watches his wife walk away from him, he feels like he did in Marsh that day, trailing behind one of them, desperate to get a look at her from the front without even knowing why. He, of course, knows what his wife looks like, but in that moment, he still needs to see her. He pushes forward, but Ryan is clogging up the hallway. Liam follows them out the door and down the driveway.

As they reach the car, he moves around Ryan and grabs for Wendy's arm. He knows then whose face he's been chasing down all those aisles to get a look at. It's not a dark-haired mystery woman near the bin of Cadbury Eggs. It's not Debbie across the street, whose light has gone out along with her plans to organize a block party tomorrow that will never happen, and it's not Kylie, who is nothing more than meaningless history and whose double-clasp bra is being safe-cracked by somebody else these days.

It's the one who rides shotgun in his Fiat convertible and howls at the sky passing by overhead, the one who collapses into his lap after she gets done jogging, with neither of them caring about her flooding sweat onto him, the one who still plays the piccolo that she used to play for the high school band but now only strangles out notes for him as they eat eggs on Saturday morning together in their dinky apartment kitchen, the one who puts on a cheerleading outfit she purchased at a costume store some Halloween and performs made-up cheers in their living room, though she never was a cheerleader, as he watches spellbound until she takes mercy on him and tugs him back to their bedroom. It's the one who, after her father died, Liam held through the darkness of five straight nights as she tried to cry away all those memories, but each time the sun came up, was able to dry up enough to hold her daughter and explain where grandpa was and what happens when a person dies.

Wendy opens the back door for Miranda and helps her inside. It's the one who stays propped up on death-defying

171

heels that elevate her above her kids and husband, in control and fully capable of steering this ship, though her muscles and everything holding her upright is dissolving fast beneath her. Liam turns her around, sure he's finally found her after so long. In the dark, he can't tell who it is, though. Then she speaks. "You got the keys, right? Drive us to the ER."

He holds the keys out for her to show her that, yes, he has them, but then he gives them to her. He'll go with them. Sure. He's their father; he needs to be there, but tonight about all he can do is come along for the ride.

She takes the keys and says nothing. She knows her husband by now, knows that when he disappears, he's only up to one thing. And she knows that as far as taking the wheel, as far as driving this car where it needs to go, he's in absolutely no condition to, and maybe never will be.

Goodbye Saturday Night

ive-year-old Johnny Jacobs has already hoisted himself halfway up into the frozen food bin at the back of Eisner by the time his mother notices, is balancing along the side, curls bouncing as he admires the rows of Gorton's fish sticks, one hand pawing through the boxes to get a handhold and one leg slung up and over the glass-paneled side, the toe of his red Keds stomping over the face of the fisherman America has trusted since 1849.

"*Holy Crap*. What have you got yourself into? Just like your father, climbing into places you don't belong." Michelle wrenches her son free from the side of the bin, and puts him back on the floor, taking one of the boxes of fish sticks, but not the one stamped with the cindery footprint. "Someday you'll be climbing in the back window of a stereo store without considering that maybe the place has an alarm system." She tosses the box into a cart which, so far, only contains a box of beef patties and a couple of Tony's pizzas. She's just begun to shop this Saturday evening.

The kid spots something at the other end of the aisle near the bleeping registers. She seizes the shoulder of his Ben 10 shirt to get his attention. "Now you stay right here next to Mommy. Don't you even think about bolting on me."

He's not even supposed to be here, is supposed to be staying with her upstairs neighbors, Hank and Janice Smitty, where he spends every Saturday night while she does her grocery shopping, not to mention every Tuesday through Friday when she waitresses until 2 AM at the Boar's Head Tavern and has to creep into their apartment, left unlocked for

173

her, and through the darkness while everybody is asleep, to retrieve Johnny from their couch and bring him, weepy and tussling, back to her place to sleep the rest of the night in his own bed. She supposes she could leave him at the Smittys' until morning. Hank and Janice wouldn't mind, and it'd be easier on both the boy and her, but there's something important about where you wake up, she knows, in helping you to understand where in this world you belong. Johnny is the closest thing Hank and Janice will ever come to having their own kid around, what with all those kinks in her plumbing, and they normally never refuse to take him when Michelle has something else going on, even for just a night, to get out from under it for a while. This weekend, though, her neighbors, who own matching Triumph cycles, decided to ride their weekend pipes up to Galena to catch the tail end of Bike Week so they can pretend to be hellraising riders instead of a pot-bellied plumber and a washed-out high school English teacher whose hellraising days, if they ever even lived them, are long gone. They really hated to miss out on two nights with their sweetie, but Bike Week is only once a year, and soon they will have to put their bikes into storage for the winter to endure another five months of the purgatory that is driving an automobile. Johnny being along once in a while is for the best anyway. Michelle certainly doesn't want them to start getting the idea that he's more theirs than hers.

Maybe she should've called on Benny to play father for one measly night of his whole pathetic life, except that probably would've required her posting bail first. No thank you. So now, here's Johnny, but he isn't about to ruin her night.

Michelle wheels her cart toward the end of the aisle, towing him behind her but keeping him at arm's length because she'd spent an hour and a half getting fixed up that evening:

174

scorching her scalp with the curling iron and leaving it to throb like a snake bite, emptying a whole can of Aquanet onto her head until the loops were encased in a caramelized crust that sit atop her head like a crown, and squeezing her can into the denim skirt that she should've said goodbye to along with her twenties but is going to wear for one last dance, the seams creaking as she moves inside it like the wooden beams of a dying ship.

A mountain of Toastette Pastries is piled at the end of the aisle, the price of $1.19 scrawled in magic marker on a round sign at the bottom, along with the slogan *For a Breakfast on the Run*. As they pass, Johnny rips the sign free from the masking tape loops securing it, sending it saucering across her path toward the meat counter.

Michelle high steps to avoid it, the stiletto heels of her Candies clicking on the tile floor, and her rhinestone anklet sparking under the fluorescents. She rounds the corner where she nearly rams the peppery-haired man wearing a short-sleeved white shirt and sandpaper tie. He's standing in front of the tortillas and punching numbers with a plastic pointer into an electronic clipboard. His eyebrows could be used to brush burrs out of a horse's hide.

His forehead compacts into ribs when he sees her. He drops the pointer and leaves it dangling there on a thread. "Michelle. Did you scare me. You look…"

He leans back to find the perfect word, but she could be waiting all night. "Stan." She averts her eyes to peer over his shoulder down the international food aisle. Before working here, Stan was some hotshot stockbroker until his wife took off on him one day, and he suffered a colossal nervous breakdown. He never could pick the winners after that, and he ended up losing all his clients' money, his job, his window office, and his company car not long after.

Michelle met him when he'd just started working here and still called this a 'bridge', talked about how he was going to start over by attending some TV-advertised tech school to become a robotics expert, make way more money than he ever had moving stocks, and actually create the future in the process, something so much more important than reinvested dividends and unrealized gains. That was eight years ago.

Now he's the man in charge during the evenings. Stan's face learned to darken like a Hispanic's from broiling his days away in the Aruba sun, where he spent the whole month of January every year he was still raking it in. Now she only sees that color in him during July when, before his second shift, he absorbs the Illinois sun all day from the balcony of his apartment. That richness in his face upon returning from Aruba probably made him look so vital, powerful, and even good enough looking, but since then, the sun has been carving deeper and deeper into his complexion with each successive year. The tan now seeps into his skin like the final blotchy brown of autumn leaves as they turn into parchment that will shatter to the touch or fall away from the branches, right around the time of year that the color falls away from Stan's cheeks, leaving him looking as rutty and grey as the bark left behind on the empty trees that crack the landscape, all of them waiting for the sun to finally return to bring them to life again.

"Hey, I didn't see you last week."

"I saw you." She steps toward the gap he's left in the aisle, but he squats in front of Johnny.

"This your boy? You ever bring him in before?"

"Nope." Chuck Hatford is cashiering in lane one. Is that an earring? She can see it flapping there on the end of his lobe. Whose skirt is he trying ruffle with that one?

"Freckle cheeks. Looks a lot like my younger one." He takes hold of the kid's arm and squints into Johnny's face as if trying to recognize something in the matrix of pores. Johnny roils inside the grip until he's let loose to dangle again from his mother's hand. Stan stands up. "Of course, he's not too young anymore. Going to be a freshman at Knox College next year. Can you wrap your head around that? You remember when he was still in middle school and scared of girls?"

"Not really." She does recall going with Stan and his two boys to some rusty carnival where she listened to his two whine the whole time about 'can they ride this' and 'can they play that', for which Daddy only managed a momentary backbone before giving in, still trying to buy back the love lost from the split-up.

"I sure love 'em when they're little with little problems. You think it'll get easier, but it never does."

Michelle jerks Johnny to get him to stop pulling. "I'll be glad when I don't have to be shackled to him all the time."

"You'll miss this." He looks down at the kid.

She turns the cart away from him. "Fat fucking chance." Doesn't need anything in this aisle anyway.

"Hey, Michelle," he calls after. "I'm sorry."

"Jesus, give it a rest. Ancient history."

"I just thought—"

He's always thinking. By some kind of miracle, he doesn't follow her to the next aisle. Johnny is trying to get away, tugging and twisting at her hand as if they're doing the Watusi. Finally, she lets him go, and he wanders away down

177

the aisle, looking back a few times before turning the corner on his way to who knows where.

She picks up a can of peas and holds it up to her face, peers past the fine print to observe the guy shelving jars of applesauce. He's new. She pinches a corkscrew of blonde hair between her fingers, tugging it down between her eyes before letting it bounce back in place with an Aquanet elasticity.

He's decked out in the Eisner's uniform: brown polyester flared pants, brown on brown plaid tie, and a short-sleeved button-down shirt with white collar flaps wide enough to reach his armpits. He finishes putting away one case of jars, breaks down the box, and slices open the next with a utility knife from his back pocket. His blonde hair hasn't been washed in a couple of weeks and dumps down onto his shoulders in clumps that eventually might develop into dreadlocks, but for now just look like gnawed away corn cobs.

Michelle shoves the can of peas down on the nearest shelf between two cans of cranberry sauce before pushing up the aisle toward him. She abandons her cart in the middle of the aisle so that the bald-headed guy behind her with the strapped-on glasses has to stop, walk around the front of his cart, and roll hers to the side to get his own past.

She reads his tag: Dan. Dan looks up when she gets within a foot of his shelving. "You got the cinnamon kind?" she asks.

He has a scabbed-over pimple on his cheekbone he must've popped this morning, and probably squirted the mirror doing it. "Cinnamon?"

"That's my favorite." She almost adds that it's her kid's favorite too, but saves herself.

Dan tears off one of the box flaps, and retrieves a jar like somebody who doesn't know what he has. His wrists are

178

thick enough for her to wrap her fist around without her fingers touching on the other side, and his heavy forearms are wormed with veins that she could've traced with her fingertips in the dark. Maybe he plays football and pumps concrete weights in his bedroom every after day after school so he doesn't get broken in two on the field, except that hair probably couldn't fit inside a football helmet. More likely he clutches drumsticks in some garage band, and chops his way through a list of cover songs so he and his buddies can one day play at some backyard party for a whole lot of dippy girls guaranteed to lift their skirts for any group of hacks on a stage with instruments in hand, even if that stage is nothing but a concrete patio next to some kid's sandbox, and the instruments sound like a handful of forks getting ground up in a disposal.

He gapes at the label and mumbles that they just have plain. His breath smells sooty. She's probably caught him right after he sneaked a smoke in the break room out back that is supposed to be nonsmoking. "Chunky style, though," he says, holding the label half for her to see and half for him to read. "Says here, 'It's like eating apples from the tree'."

"You're quite a salesman, but if I wanted apples from the tree, I'd go to an orchard."

He looks again to make sure all the jars are the same. Then he finally steers away from the labels to observe the narrow red and white stripes running up and down her tank top like some optical illusion that will turn into a pirate ship or bouquet of flowers if he stares long enough. The bald guy lags near the spinach to get a look too.

"The plain tastes so bland. Reminds me of—" She finishes with a giggle. "Maybe you got some out back." There are no jars out back. Of that, she is sure.

He glances over to the registers and then back to the meat counter as if ascertaining where the hidden stock might be. This one. Stan must make him load shelves because he doesn't possess the grey matter for anything else, probably hands him the box cutter and prays the kid clocks out at the end of the night with both hands still attached. Still, you can't hold those forearms against him, or those eyes the color of a Caribbean Ocean, albeit only as deep as the water a foot from shore.

"Forget it." If she sends him on an errand, he may never find his way back. She reaches over and lifts the jar from his hands, her fingers the same color as the applesauce inside. "I've never had this kind, and I'll try anything once." The bald guy parked her cart on the other side of the aisle out of her reach, so she just cradles the jar in her hands, flicking at the peeled-up corner of the label with her Petunia Pink fingernail. "When did you start here?"

"Only about a month ago, but I don't usually work Saturdays." He's back to examining her stripes.

"Eisner is like a disco apocalypse," she says. She runs her knuckles down the front of his God-awful tie to smooth it out. Somebody's been folding it up and stuffing it into his back pocket after he gets off, probably sits on it the whole way home. When she gets to the bottom, she tweezes the tip between her fingernails and leaves a crescent-shaped crimp behind in the polyester. What a little boy. "Looks like you got a case of Saturday Night Fever."

He glances down at himself and plucks the leg of his pants. "They're like wearing sandpaper. I could start myself on fire." He produces a sluggish grin to conceal the staleness of what he said, somebody who doesn't know how to deliver a joke, maybe his only joke, something he's told to every

180

coworker and every other customer he's talked to since he started. Doesn't she feel special?

"Occupational hazard," she says. A woman with a cheque book in one hand and a fistful of coupons in the other comes down the aisle. As she rolls her cart past, she inventories Michelle from attic to basement.

"What time do they let you peel yourself out of this turd suit anyway?" When he doesn't answer right away, she asks, "What time are you off tonight?"

He tucks his hair behind his ears like a girl might do, exposing his pasty, pitted cheeks. "Nine. I've had to pick up some extra hours." He drops his voice. "On account of that guy blowing his head off."

"What?" She absently grasps onto the closest shelf and takes a clopping step back.

"Shot himself."

"What guy? Who're you talking about? Somebody who worked here?"

He waits until the coupon lady moseys her way out of earshot, and he lowers his voice even more before continuing. Michelle has to lean in to hear, her snaky curls nearly touching his forehead. "Greg Pollard. He bagged mostly."

"Who's Greg Pollard?"

"I only met him once, and all he ever said to me was, 'Why can't people just give it to you straight?' I wasn't even sure he was talking to me, maybe just talking to anybody or maybe thought I was somebody else. Two days later he took his dad's twenty-gauge into the bedroom closet with him." Dan begins to slice curlicues in the top of the applesauce box. "I heard he wrapped a towel around his head before he did it—

181

to hold in the mess, I guess. But I don't think it worked." He cuts a straight line in the cardboard across his artwork. "I hear they're putting the house on the market."

"I didn't hear anything about it." Her voice accelerates. "I don't know how I didn't hear anything. Wasn't even in the paper, I don't think." She doesn't get a paper, though. She clops her heeled foot against the tile again, and her inhale comes in a gasp because she forgets to breathe for a moment.

"They've been kind of trying to keep it quiet, told us not to talk about it. His mom is really wrecked about it. I saw her come in once. She got a basket, filled it up, and just all of a sudden dropped everything and ran out. I had to put it all back."

"Why?"

Amazingly, Dan figures out what she's asking about. "They don't really know. Only thing I heard is his dad split town a couple years ago, and left him and his mom behind." He turns the box on its side for more cutting room, slashes what could be a paisley or a teardrop in the box and lets the cut-out fall inside. "You'd think…after two years…he'd get over it. Everyone around here said they thought he did."

"I don't remember him," she says. Ten feet away, a fat guy in a cardigan sweater is checking the calorie content of crinkle-cut carrots. "How long did he work here?"

"Over three years, I think."

"Did he work Saturday nights?"

"Yeah, now we got to cover all his hours."

"Too fucking bad for you. What did he look like?"

She steps on her toes to peer over Dan's shoulder, but she can't see past the man whose sweater won't even button around his belly. She can't see any other stock boys, and she can't see who is bagging or cashiering in the third lane up front.

Eisner has mostly boys. She knows their names if they work the weekend—Chuck Hatford, Brad Williams, Frankie Dennison, Jeff Uftrinct. She should've known them all. How, after coming to shop here almost every Saturday night off for the past three years, could she have possibly missed a boy named Greg Pollard every single time? Maybe he worked customer service, cloistered in that booth all night, inaccessible unless she wanted change for a twenty.

"Short guy." It's all the description Dan offers, but maybe it's enough. Maybe Greg was just too short to consider. Maybe if she just hadn't worn heels, if she'd just been closer to his level, if she introduced herself to him some Saturday, just once, and they got to talking about applesauce or apricots or music or whatever he wanted to talk about.

She locks back on Dan. "What did you say you were doing after?"

"After what?"

"After work. What are you doing after work?" Before Michelle receives an answer, a tug comes on the back of her skirt. She turns to see that Johnny is back, and he's been busy. He grins up at her with chocolate lipstick spread across his face out to his cheekbones. His hands are coated with it up to his wrists, probably from digging his way through a bulk bin of Raisinets or Sno-Caps.

"What have you done now?" She doesn't really want to know the answer, sure doesn't want Dan to know. Johnny won't answer anyway. No worry about that. He lets loose of her skirt, leaving a semisweet handprint behind on the denim. "You little dink. Just look what you did to me."

183

She reaches in her purse for something to wipe it off, but all she finds is a $200 deposit receipt from the last time she got paid. She licks the back, tasting the graphite of the bank printer, and swabs at the stain, only succeeding in mashing it down into the braids of denim stitching. "I can't believe what you put me through. I could wring your neck. I could wring your bloody neck."

Stooping down, she starts in on him with the receipt, scrubbing at the chocolate around his mouth. He swivels his head and tugs to get away from her, but she hooks her free arm around his back, corralling him there. "You stay still." He doesn't. *"Stay still."*

His eye bulges and sags as she scours his chunky left cheek. The chocolate is too dry to come off, and there isn't enough spit on the receipt to liquefy it again, but she keeps rubbing up and down his cheek like somebody sanding the corner of an unfinished table to grind away the ridges.

His eyes float. "Just stop it. See what being bad gets you. You're stealing, you know that? I'm not paying for—" The tears begin to provide the moisture she needs. A portion of chocolate wipes away, but the receipt disintegrates into snowflakes in her hand. She drops it to the floor. "Fine. You'll just have to be that way until we get home. I can't get you any better than that." The rest of the chocolate is still all around his mouth, but the left side is hidden underneath the red scuffs.

She unhooks her arm from him, but he hesitates, then holds open his hand to show her a roll of Wint-O-Green Lifesavers, the foil wrapper dented and unraveling at one end.

"Are you kidding me? No way. You've had enough for tonight. Put them back where you found them."

Johnny flops to his knees on the floor, and erupts into waves of bawling that crash through the aisles like a siren warning them of impending doom.

"Put them back." Her voice slows and elevates at the same time. *"You put them back right now."*

Johnny cradles the roll in his lap and covers it with both hands, probably thinking she will forget he ever showed them to her, and maybe she will. Michelle stands up to tell Dan that he doesn't need to worry, that he won't have to put up with any of this tonight. She can drop Johnny at another neighbor's. There must be other people living around her who want them but can't have them, or don't mind one more, or miss having a young one around since all theirs left home. There's got to be somebody who will give her and Dan the rest of the night to themselves.

He is halfway up the aisle, though, tugging the cart of boxes toward the front of the store. One wheel of the cart whammers back and forth because something in its mechanisms has been bent, preventing it from rolling a calm straight line. She can't help but think of parents' day at the nursery school, where all the kids were obediently sitting at their miniature desks waiting for their parents to see all the uppercase letters they'd written and crayon pictures they'd drawn, except her Johnny, who was tearing around the room as if it were time to play tag or jet airplane, and howling something that sounded somewhat like a jet engine but nothing close to words. He was oblivious to Mrs. Eckoff imploring him to please sit down, her hands held up in front of her as if bracing for an impact, was oblivious to the twelve sets of parents aghast at his behavior, and was oblivious to Michelle, who'd left the pack of parents on the side to call to him. "Johnny, you sit down. Johnny, you sit down now like Mrs.

Eckoff said." He didn't sit down, not until Michelle hauled him to his seat, shoving him down when he tried to get back up, and having to stand there between the desks with a fist on each shoulder. Mrs. Eckoff sped up her welcome speech, knowing Johnny couldn't be kept down for long, and the other parents tried to pay attention, but kept dodging their focus to Johnny and loving theirs just a little bit more.

She turns on Johnny now. "You see?" she says. "You see what you did?" He is staring down into his lap at his chocolate-dipped fingers. "What you do every time I take you anywhere?" He isn't crying anymore, just sniffling a little.

She hooks her hands underneath his arms and lifts him until he puts his feet down. "Listen to me, goddamn it, *listen to me.*" The man who decided crinkle-cut carrots weren't too fattening for him is now finding out about creamed corn. He looks up to see what all the shouting is about. As Michelle locks eyes on him, he abruptly dumps the can into his cart and continues down the aisle onto the next.

"You see?" He doesn't see, won't see, won't even look up at her. She gives him a jiggle, but it doesn't get his attention, so she strikes his cheek with the backside of her hand. It's the only way to get through. His head wrenches right and knocks into the cans of beets. It takes a second. Then he begins to wail.

"Oh stop it. I'm sorry. I didn't mean to hit you so hard. I didn't hit you that hard." The package of Lifesavers drops to the floor and rolls between her legs. He brings both hands up to his cheek, but never touches it, just cups them over the impact point as he elevates his screams to bloody murder.

Michelle brings him into her, but he only wrestles in her arms. She glances up toward the front where Gail is ringing up in three, her hair shaved to fuzz on one side to reveal her triple pierced ear. Her boyfriend, Bobby Tingston, is her

186

bagger. What he sees in that punky skank, Michelle will never understand. The two of them should be working on the woman's groceries lined up on the conveyor, but they've stalled in unison to watch down seven.

"You quit it," she whispers into his ear. "You quit it, or no TV when we get home. I promise you that." She releases him, and he keeps on, freezing the rest of the shoppers with his bray. He probably never would've quit except he runs out of breath just then. He huffles for air, shivers, and slurps up the tears, snot, and drool coating his lips.

"Do you see now?" He tries to fall to his knees again, but she catches his wrist and keeps him on his feet.

Someone has come up the aisle behind her. "Is he all right?"

Michelle doesn't answer or look back. She leaves her cart sitting next to the string beans, and marches Johnny up toward the front, yanking his arm every few steps to keep him walking, like fighting the bad wheel on a shopping cart.

At the front, Bobby and his freakshow girlfriend have started on the groceries, but he isn't looking to see what he's putting into bags, milk stacked right on top of bread. She isn't looking to see what she's running over the scanner, just sort of flipping each thing over and over until she gets a beep.

Dan parked his cart next to the customer service desk and is a few feet away talking to seventeen-year-old Steve Draper, who is shelving bottles of root beer and who Michelle met during a shopping trip a couple of months ago. They cease talking as she shoves Johnny by.

She heads for the way out, passing Chuck cashiering in the first lane. He doesn't have a customer, but is tapping on the register keys as if ringing something in. She's within three feet of him, but he doesn't say a word, doesn't even glance up.

187

It is an earring, a crucifix. Is he kidding? She has just triggered the motion detector that causes the glass doors to swing open when someone grabs the back of her arm. She stops with a smile ready until he steps in front of her.

"You can't do that," Stan says. "You can't do that in the store…to your boy."

Michelle waits there for him to say something else, but he doesn't say another thing. Somebody forgot the deodorant this morning. She yanks her arm, but his fingers have already left her. She heads outside, letting the doors close behind her and seal in the stink.

Her cabinets are still empty, and she left without getting a goddamn thing. Tomorrow she'll have to go shopping with Johnny in tow down at the Eagle on Route 55, where the employees consist almost entirely of geriatrics and stupid, gum-cracking girls, on a Sunday afternoon when anybody that age has nothing to think about except the dreaded inevitability of school the next day.

She stands Johnny up against the 7-UP machine out front, his head knocking the pane of plastic hard enough for the inner fluorescent lamp to blink, too hard for what he had done really, too hard for anything he could've done, and realizing that somehow makes her want to do it to him again. "You see now? I can never go back there. I can never go back. You see what you did?"

He stares down at the tops of his sneakers, isn't going to answer her, has maybe a twelve-word vocabulary at his disposal, but isn't going to use any of them now. She leaves him there and wanders to the curb, glancing across the parking lot at her yellow Hyundai Sonata with the rust patch on the side panel and the taped-over taillight. She remembers the day she bought it outright, seven years ago after her measly divorce settlement finally arrived from her husband, the man who was unable to honor anything in their marriage aside from her refusal to have kids. Two years later came Johnny.

How she had torn out of that dealership, squealing the tires on the only new car she would ever own in her life, and so much open road ahead of her. She never could have done that now. The Hyundai's transmission is going. Each time she shifts, the gears feel like crumbling cheese. Someday soon, the bottom is going to drop out, fall out right onto the road and halt that car forever. But not yet, probably not for at least a thousand miles of road ahead of her.

Acknowledgements

Thanks to Kate Fitzpatrick, a wonderful colleague and master of literature who helped me edit these pieces and get a handle on my out of control sentences. It's been great working with you and being your friend all these years.

Thank you to my son Jack for bringing the cover to life through his drawing and technical artistry. He has vision and talent I wish I had.

Thanks to my wife Debbie, who is eternally supportive of me no matter how many hours I spend in my office cave and no matter how poor my time management is. She has the sharpest mind I know and is not afraid to be honest with me about my work, no matter how I might take it. I always thought a writer needed to be miserable to keep coming up with material to write about, but she has made me understand you can be blissfully happy and still find the words.

About The Author

Joseph Kraus teaches creative writing, English, and debate at Portsmouth High School in New Hampshire as well as coaches the debate team which recently competed in Harvard's National Speech and Debate Tournament. He completed his Masters of Arts in Fiction Writing from the University of New Hampshire where he was awarded both the Elizabeth Jones Scholarship and the Dick Shea Memorial Prize for his writing. He resides in Portsmouth with his wife and two boys. His work shows influences of his midwestern upbringing and has been published in a variety of literary outlets including *The Binnacle* and *Scars Publishing*.

www.ingramcontent.com/pod-product-compliance
Lightning Source LLC
Chambersburg PA
CBHW051119260626
47170CB00005B/1579